FELICITY AND JASON
A Southern Love Story
2

A Novel By

TABEITHA POLLARD

Royalty Publishing House is now accepting manuscripts from aspiring or experienced urban romance authors!

WHAT MAY PLACE YOU ABOVE THE REST:

Heroes who are the ultimate book bae: strong-willed, maybe a little rough around the edges but willing to risk it all for the woman he loves.

Heroines who are the ultimate match: the girl next door type, not perfect - has her faults but is still a decent person. One who is willing to risk it all for the man she loves.

The rest is up to you! Just be creative, think out of the box, keep it sexy and intriguing!

If you'd like to join the Royal family, send us the first 15K words (60 pages) of your completed manuscript to submissions@royaltypublishinghouse.com

Acknowledgements

First of all, I want to thank each and every one of you that has taken the time to read one of my books. You all mean so much to me to ride this ride with me. This journey is a lifelong one and it doesn't end because a book is over. Like the late Nipsey Hussle always said—The Marathon Continues.

To my ride or dies. Frances, Denora, Steven, Ayesha, Elena and Erin. Y'all are the real MVPs because none of you switched up on a chick even when I was in my feelings like Drake. You stood by me and waited for me to get back on my act right and bust out these keys.

To the folks that have recently come in my life and helped motivate me. Michelle Davis. Woman, thank you so much. When I reached out to you with my personal issues, you prayed for me and kept me encouraged. You are the main reason I was able to finish this book. Thank you so much for all that you do.

Annitia, girl where would I be without your accountability and word count challenges. That kept me going when I felt like giving up. Not to mention you're such a dope ass writer.

Porscha, you took a chance on me and thank you for allowing me to venture into the urban romance genre. You believed that I could do it when I was unsure that I could. I thought my writing career was over, but now it has new life and I am forever grateful.

To my kids and the newest member to my household, my nephew. I love you all and I am so grateful to call my nephew my son now. I will do all I can to make you all proud of me.

And to any one of you that I didn't mention_____, thank you so much for all of your support!

Stay Divine!
Tabeitha Pollard.
#itsapollardthing

Synopsis

Felicity is once again back in the headlines and it isn't all good. After Dylan decided to kiss her in front of a fan looking for something juicy, Jason is now questioning her loyalty to him. She knows that she hasn't done anything wrong, but Jason's trust issues may prove to be too much for her. Will he be able to handle it when she tells him that Dylan wants to be a part of Avalon's life?

Jason thought that he had the perfect relationship. That was until Dylan found a way to place doubt in his mind. Jason knew that he had been burned before and he promised himself that he would never let another woman play him. Will his jealous ways push the woman of his dreams away, or will he wake up and realize that everything isn't what it seems?

Dylan is obsessed with getting Avalon and Felicity back. He wants what he wants, and no one is going to stop him. He plans on stopping at nothing short of murder to get Felicity back in his bed and Avalon to call him Daddy. Not even his parents or threats on his career will stop him. Will he take it one step too far, or will he succeed in his quest for love?

Raven is back and with a vengeance. Seeing everyone going so hard for Felicity makes her blood boil. She wants Felicity to be a vague memory in everyone's eyes and plans on using her new husband to do it. She wants everyone to suffer and she knows that Felicity's disappearance will cause everyone pain. A plot to kidnap the singer will cause an entire city to almost burn. Will this be the end of Raven, or will this be her rise to the top?

So many lives, so little time. When those lights come on, what will happen? Is it all for show, or is this real life? Find out what happens in this chilling finale!

Felicity

I couldn't believe that this dumb ass just kissed me. As soon as his lips touched mine, I pulled back and slapped his ass so hard, I was sure his mama felt it. That was so disrespectful because he was just so sincere and apologetic a moment before. I didn't have time for his bipolar bullshit, and I knew that the person that was on the curb probably took a few pictures. This would be all over the blogs by morning and now I had to explain this shit to Jason before shit hit the fan.

"Don't you ever again in life pull that shit. Now I have to do fucking damage control because you want to be sneaky like your ex-bitch! Get the fuck out my car. And don't worry about that money. It was only pocket change," I spat.

Dylan climbed out of my car and gave me a look like he wanted to say something. I sucked my teeth and pulled off, barely giving him a chance to close my door and back away from the curb. I couldn't believe that I let myself get sucked into his bullshit once again. I straight beat myself up all the way home because of it. I pulled into my garage and sat in my car for a few minutes after I turned it off. I wanted to pull back out and run away, but I wasn't a scared bitch by any means.

I got out and went into the house feeling like I wanted to shit on myself. Jason was the biggest gentleman that I knew, but if pushed, his hood side would rear its ugly head. I damn sure didn't want to be the one on the receiving end of his wrath. But like Miss Gina always said, it was better to hear the truth from that person than out in the street where the message gets lost in translation.

"You made it back safe. Anything happen?" Jason asked when I walked through the door. He was fixing himself and Avalon bowls of cereal since I wasn't there to get breakfast going.

"Yeah, and I need to talk to you about it before it hits the blogs," I said and then explained to him about Dylan trying to hold my hand at the jail, all the way down to the kiss he forced on me.

When I say that Jason's face turned dark, I meant that shit literally. It was like all the blood in his body went right to his face making it change color right before my eyes. I wanted to run through the walls to get away from this nigga because he was scaring my ass. He didn't say a word for about two minutes.

"His career is over. I was going to release his album, but that shit won't see the light of day now. He fucked up for real," Jason said.

He picked up his phone and left me standing there shaking like a leaf in a tornado. I didn't know if I should follow him or stay put. I chose the latter and tried to focus on my daughter who was too busy reading in her Kindle to pay us any attention. I sat down across from her to get her attention.

"Are you ready for your first day of school on Monday?" I asked her.

"I guess so. At least Juliette will be in the same class as me and she and Clark can ride the bus with me," she said. Ione was going to middle school this year and the girls weren't happy that they were being separated.

"You do know that you will see Ione after school, right?" I reassured her.

"Good, because I know she don't like the girls in her class. She said that they all think they're better than her because Miss Ginger is a nurse and their parents are lawyers and doctors," Avalon told me.

I felt bad for the girls because bullying was no joke. Kids were killing themselves younger and younger every day because people didn't teach their kids how much words could hurt. I remember the first time a bitch came out her mouth wrong to me about having a baby when I was in the ninth grade. I beat her ass so bad that I thought I was going to juvie. But no one said anything else about it after that, either.

"Well, sugar, you just remember that words hurt more than physical beatings. No one forgets what was being said about them. It takes years to regain any confidence that you lose when people don't know how to keep their mouths shut. As long as you know how special you are and you don't do that to others, we're good," I explained.

"But what if one of those raggedy things says something to me or tries to hit me?" she asked. I had to laugh because she got that shit from Miss Gina.

"You roast the hell out of their ass. And if they try and fight you, take the biggest book you can find and rearrange their face. And that is only if the teachers don't do anything to stop them," I told her.

"Okay, Mommy. And you need to put money in the swear jar. Jason, too," she told me.

My daughter made us take one of the large, empty pickle jars and put twenty dollars in it every time she caught us cussing. Whenever it got full, I was to put the money in a bank account for her. That little girl already had over five thousand dollars in it because we couldn't watch our mouths. She was about to be one wealthy child before she got to middle school, the little hustler.

"Can I go and play with the girls?" she asked me. I told her to call Ginger and make sure it was okay and to have Ione come and walk her over. She took off to make her call just as Jason walked back in the kitchen.

"Jason, I'm so sorry. I would have never left out to help that bastard if I had known," I started. He put his hand up to stop me from talking.

"Look, I don't know what all went down, but I know you. You came and told me right away and that says a lot. But let's be clear. I don't want him anywhere near you or Avalon. His white ass has an agenda. He was with Raven for a long ass time and there is no way that her ways didn't rub off on his gullible ass," he warned.

"I don't know about that since he is Avalon's father. I really don't want to deny her a relationship with him if he wants to step up. That wouldn't be fair to my daughter. You gotta know that," I pleaded.

"Where the fuck was his ass when you were struggling? That muhfucka ain't send you one fucking dime in damn near nine years and now you want to be on some kumbaya shit. Fuck outta here," he argued back.

"What's this really about Jason? Are you really that insecure that you think that I would do you like that gold-digging ass cum bucket Raven? Do you really think I'm that low? Because if you do, nigga, you must be on crack," I spat back.

I couldn't believe that we were actually in my kitchen going back and forth like we didn't know each other. It was unbelievable what could happen in just a span of a few short hours. Jason had me and the game all fucked up if he thought for one second that he was going to talk to me any old kind of way. I wasn't his ex-wife or any of those random hoes he was sticking his dick in. He was about to learn about me really quick.

"I'm not a nigga that's insecure about shit. I can get any bitch I want. I just don't trust this man. And that kiss looked real fucking bad, I'm not even gonna front. I do feel some type of way about that shit," he admitted.

"What was it that you told me? That as long as you know the real, we don't have to worry about the blogs and shit. And don't even worry, I already texted your mom and Pamela. They've been on damage control since I almost ran Dylan's ass over," I told him.

When he looked at me funny, I told him the part I didn't get to about me pulling off with him still holding the door to my car. Jason looked at me with his mouth open at first, and then busted out laughing a second later. He was laughing so hard that our argument was forgotten just that fast.

"Man, remind me to never piss you off. And don't be fucking up that car. Shit damn near ran me dry, Maria Andretti," he joked.

"One, your ass will never be broke. Two, I know how to handle that car. Three, you now owe me and the girls a day at the spa. Questioning my ass and shit," I said.

"Swear jar!" we both said the same time and we put five hundred apiece inside because we literally cussed more than sailors at Fleet Week.

I was about to kiss Jason, but my doorbell rang and then I heard Ginger's loud ass. She was walking in with the girls all dressed up and I had forgotten all about going out with everybody that day. With all of the arguing Jason and I had just been doing and Dylan's bullshit, I had forgotten all about the outing.

"I know your ass better be getting dressed. You look like you ready to ask niggas for money on the corner," her ass had the nerve to say.

"Kiss my ass. I'll be ready in thirty minutes. We had a lot going on here," I explained.

"It's all good. I saw all that shit on The Shade Room. I had to go in on a few of them bald headed ass wombats up there. Told them about themselves in English and in Spanish in case they couldn't understand me in English," her ass had the nerve to say.

I couldn't do shit but laugh at her ass. She was one chick that you never wanted to piss off. Her ass would roast you so bad, your enemies felt bad for you. I was ready to see what she said, but I needed to wash my ass and get dressed. It was time for us to go out, have fun and forget about the bullshit that just went on.

Jason

I didn't want to come across as a jealous ass nigga, but that shit hit a nigga hard when I saw that picture. Dylan wanted more than just a relationship with his daughter: he wanted my woman. And there was no way in hell that I was going to just roll over and let him take either of them away from me.

"So, what are you going to do about Dylan? I don't like his ass and I haven't ever been in the same room as him," Ginger said, breaking me from my thoughts.

"Can't let anyone in on this. The less people that know, the better," I said and then went into the room with Felicity.

When I saw her bent over in her white lace boy shorts, my dick rocked all the way up. Her ass was sitting up like a bubble and her panties were getting lost in all of that cinnamon goodness she was toting. I wanted to stay mad at her, but after what she told me about nearly running Dylan over and the way she was looking, I couldn't help myself. I walked up to her and grabbed a handful of her ass.

"Not now. We got people waiting on us and the last thing I want to hear is Ginger's mouth. Especially when she finds out Kente is coming with us. Can you hand me my shoes?" she whined and moved out of my reach.

"Damn, a nigga can't even get a little cheek action. Blocking ass friends," I joked loud enough for Ginger to hear.

"Uh-uh, don't do me! Fefe, get your man!" Ginger yelled back. Felicity and I both laughed and finished getting dressed.

We came out the room just as Kwame, Megan, Kente and their kids came through the door. Very few people knew that Kente had a son that he was raising on his own. His son's mother died from complications during the c-section with him. She developed two blood clots that took her and Lyndon's twin from them.

"Who is this good-looking guy?" Felicity asked, completely ignoring Kente.

"I'm Lyndon Marquise Bintu. I'm six and I like Pokémon," Lyndon said, and I swear every woman's heart melted right in front of us.

"Well, I guess us men just got left. My nephew is that dude!" Kwame joked.

We laughed and piled into the kitchen where there was a spread set up. As soon as Felicity got that call the night before, I called my personal chef to whip us up brunch. Felicity wanted to do it herself, but circumstances changed, and we had to improvise.

"Look, I need to tell you all something," Kente spoke up while we were eating.

"What's up?" I asked.

"It's about Dylan. I don't even feel right politicking with all of you knowing what I know. The nigga is bugged out," he started.

"You better start talking, and fast. Anything about him concerns my daughter," Felicity demanded.

"He's been using me to try and get information about you guys. He's pissed because you haven't released his EP and then you're with Fefe. He thinks that you stole his girl or some shit. Dude claims he's still in love with you and shit. He's been doing nothing but drinking lean and popping pills all day. I can't even get his ass in the studio sober," he admitted to us.

"I knew it! His dumb ass. I can't believe this shit. Babe, change your number or block his ass on everything. He thinks I fucked his life up. He has no idea how fucked up it can get," I spat.

"Baby, I need you to stay calm and let's forget about Dylan for the day," Felicity said and touched me gently on the arm.

I swear that one touch was enough to stop me from grabbing my steel and putting two hot ones in Dylan's head. There was something calming about her that made me want to be a better man for her. I wanted to protect her and Avalon. I wanted to give them the life that they had been robbed of and deserved. I knew that I had to get my feelings in check before I lost the best thing that ever happened to me.

We decided to let the situation with Dylan stay at the house because the Sprinters were pulling up to the house. I decided to have the kids and nannies in one van and the adults in the other. That way we could talk freely without having to watch how we spoke in front of the kids. That, and we wouldn't have to worry about setting cash aside for Avalon's swear jar. That girl was about to be able to pay for four years at Dartmouth if she kept that jar going.

"I'm trying to figure out where the hell Raven's ass disappeared to," Kwame spoke up as soon as we pulled off.

"Her pops got her hidden somewhere in the city. I lost track of her ass after they fled Colombia. She don't even know that she has a big ass target on her back because of her dad," I explained.

I told them all about her father's shady ass. The man would fuck over his own mama to get ahead. He tried to get me for half a million dollars when he wanted me to invest in a nice little lounge with him. My mom found out and then had a forensic accountant look into

Javad's finances. He was moving money to off-shore accounts all over the world from his business.

He would make sure that the businesses were doing well, and then after six months, business would suddenly take a turn. The business would see a sudden slow down until there would seem to be no money left. But that wasn't the case at all. He would steadily filter the revenue out in his accounts until he bled the business dry.

"Damn. That man ain't shit for that. I know I can't stand that bitch Raven, but she doesn't deserve to be a casualty in a war that her father started. You need to warn her about him," Felicity said.

"That right there is why I love your ass," I blurted out. Up until now, I had never really said the words. We just showed each other how we felt. The look on Felicity's face showed her surprise as well.

"Wait a minute! Is this the first time you heard this?" Megan asked.

"Hell yeah! This nigga don't have one romantic bone in his body," she joked.

"Well, now we got to go out and celebrate tonight! This nigga done dropped the L word! I thought that would never happen, considering your past," Ginger commented.

"Be easy on the man. It took a lot for him to even want to be with someone on a one-on-one basis," Kente said to Ginger.

When I tell you Ginger's ass got quiet, she went mute. In the time that I'd known her, I had never seen what her lips looked like when they were joined together. She was always commenting on something, but it was usually in a positive way. She had the voice and the personality for radio, and I had an audition lined up for her for a couple of radio stations in the area.

"Well, damn. I never knew your lips knew what they felt like together. I bet they're hugging like long lost relatives," Felicity joked.

"You and Jason gone quit with the jokes. I do not talk that damn much," Ginger pouted.

"You're cute when you pout," Kente said, and I swear I saw Ginger blush. Felicity's plan to get those two together seemed to be working. All they needed was the opportunity to be around each other.

The day turned out to be a good day. We took the kids to the aquarium, the zoo and skating. By the time we got back to Felicity's, the kids were worn out. We all knew that they would sleep all night. That would leave the night to us. I planned to take the adults out to Mystique and chill in the private VIP lounge. It was time for the adults to be adults and have fun.

"Damn, baby. Don't get fucked up," I said as I complimented Felicity.

She came out of the shower in a pure white bandage dress. The dress hugged every curve on her body, making that ass and titties sit up just right. The silver, open-toed stilettos made her calves look amazing. And that pedicure with the white polish had a nigga wanting to suck on her toes. Her hair was pulled up into a cute puff on top her head, and she had on a pair of diamond teardrop earrings. She had on the matching tennis bracelet and necklace to finish off her look.

I was matching her fly in a white Tom Ford suit and silver Louboutin sneakers. My hair was freshly lined up and my curls were sitting right on top. I put on my Chopard watch and grabbed my Fendi shades. I sprayed on some Creed cologne before heading out to the living room to kiss my baby girl goodnight.

"You two look sharp!" Miss Gina exclaimed when we came out the room.

"Jason, are you going to marry my mommy tonight?" Avalon asked, and I choked on my spit.

"Not tonight, sweet pea. But maybe I will one day in the future," I honestly admitted while looking back at Felicity to see her response.

She was just staring at me with a blank expression on her face. I'm sure that the argument from earlier, and me finally telling her that I loved her, had her feelings all over the place. She hadn't spoken much the entire day, and it slightly bothered me, but I was willing to let it go for the night.

"The car is waiting on us," she said softly. She walked over and kissed her daughter before taking my hand and walking out the door. We got in the car and we were silent for the first five minutes of the ride.

"Did you really mean what you said earlier?" she asked me.

"Of course, I did. I told you that I would never say anything that I don't mean. I do apologize for this morning. That shit was foul, and I shouldn't take shit out on you. That shit was meant for Dylan. I'm so sorry for that," I said.

"Oh, I know you didn't mean most of that shit. Because you wouldn't be able to see otherwise. Just start trusting me and we'll be good. But did you see the way that Kente was with Gin? I think we made a love connection," she replied with a smile.

"That shit is wild! I should have known you were up to no good, though. Kente's ass been sprung since that day she sat in your session." I wasn't lying. Kente took one look at Ginger and homeboy was ready to marry her ass right then and there.

We pulled up to the club and the paparazzi were deep as fuck. I knew they were there to try and catch us. They wanted to see if there was a rift between me and Felicity, but little did they know, we were more solid than a hundred pounds of diamonds. I looked at Felicity and she gave me a tense look before I squeezed her hand. We waited until the driver opened up the door to my Rolls Royce to step out. As soon as we did, we were hit with question after question.

"Is everything okay with you guys?"

"Is there trouble in paradise? I guess Fefe is still hung up on the white meat."

"I knew that y'all were fronting for the Gram."

"Let's be clear right now. Dylan is the past. I am her present and future. They share a child together and nothing else. And they really don't share that since she's the only one still caring for her. We're good over here, as you can clearly see. Dylan, this is for you," I barked. I pulled Felicity to me and planted a sensual kiss on her lips that left her speechless.

That also shut up the paparazzi and all of their questions. I grabbed Felicity's hand and we walked into the club with our heads held high like the royalty we were. Nothing was going to bring us down. I would make sure of that, no matter what.

Ginger

You couldn't have told me a year ago that I would be spending an entire day with THE Kente Bintu. When I say that nigga is fine, he is fine! He was a smooth, dark chocolate man with the almond-shaped hazel eyes that had these little brown flecks in them. He was about five-ten and a hundred and eighty pounds of pure steel. He had not one tattoo on his body or any fat for that matter. He had the whitest set of straight teeth that I had ever seen on a man. And that voice! Good Lord, I wanted to throw my panties down his throat the moment I heard him speak.

"Mom, be careful tonight. You know Dad is going to throw a fit when this hits the blogs," my daughter Ione advised.

"He can't be mad at me. He has a whole girlfriend at home. By the way, has he called so you can finally meet your brother?" I asked.

"Mom, really? You know that woman hates us, and he doesn't say anything about her mouth. That's why I won't go over there. I had to tell her about her edgeless self. Trying to call me out when her wig was drier than burnt toast," Ione said.

"I can't take you!" I laughed. My child was definitely all me. She looked like her father, but her mannerisms and attitude came straight from me.

"I'm just saying. I try to be respectful when I FaceTime Dad, but she is always in the back talking smack. I don't know what he sees in that wombat," she continued.

I just kept on getting ready. I didn't have much time before Kente showed up. I slid into a white lace minidress that I found on Fashion Nova and matched it with a pair of green pumps. I found my jade and gold jewelry to match. I sprayed on my Versace White Jean cologne and unwrapped my hair so that it fell down in soft waves.

I looked amazing for a woman with three kids. I was about five-three and weighed one hundred thirty-five pounds. I was stacked in the ass, but small in the breasts. I had deep tanned skin and my hair was jet black. My small, dark eyes were my best feature in my eyes. I didn't smile much because I was missing two side teeth from an accident right after I had Juliette. I was still pretty, but that was the one thing I was ashamed of.

"Don't get pregnant!" my sister Francesca said as she came in the room. She had moved in permanently with me to go to nursing school down here. She and our parents weren't getting along and I promised that I would look out for her if they let her stay with me.

"Shut up, ugly," I said back to her. She was far from ugly. In fact, we looked exactly alike, except she was super thin and tall.

"Whatever, I know I'm fine. But that piece of man candy just pulled up in a Wraith. I want to be like you when I grow up," she said wistfully.

"No. You need to focus on your career and not some nigga. Look at what I'm going through with Devante. That shit is not cute at all," I advised before I went to answer the door. I was speechless as I looked at Kente.

He was matching me, fly in a pair of white Marc Jacobs slacks, plus he had on a white collarless shirt and a pair of white Stacy Adams on his feet. He was only wearing one iced out Cuban link necklace and his Presidential Rolex. He had his long dreads pulled up into a man bun and two diamond slugs in his mouth. He had me ready to take his ass back in my bedroom and let him knock the dust off my pussy. Boy, was I glad I decided to actually wear panties for once.

"Stop eye fucking me and take these flowers, girl," he joked.

"Nobody was eye fucking anything. You look aite," I joked back as I took the daisies from him. When I did that, I noticed that he had a long velvet box in his hand.

"This is for you to wear tonight. Nobody can say that I don't know how to treat my date," he said and opened the box, revealing a jade and diamond bracelet.

"Oh my god! You didn't have to do this!" I exclaimed as he put the jewelry on me.

"Yes, the hell he did! I approve!" my sister said from behind us. I introduced them and then we headed out since we were running behind schedule.

"I like your sister. She's funny as hell. All of you are. You really need to think about what I said earlier," he said as we drove towards the club.

Kente mentioned that he was asked to be a part of *Love and Hip Hop Atlanta* and he thought that I would look good on his arm. Not to mention that it would put money in my pockets. He was already feeling me and it wouldn't be fabricated that I was his love interest because I was going to be his girl regardless. He said that I was made for television and that he wouldn't take no for an answer.

"I already told you that I'm going to think about it. I need to talk to Jason and see what he thinks and to see if his team can represent me if I do," I said.

"I can respect that. You really know about handling your business. I told you that I knew you were special from the first day I saw you. I been trying to get Fefe to hook us up. I'm telling you, you're about to be a nigga's wife," he stated.

I wasn't sure if I wanted to go down that road. I mean, Devante's broke ass dogged me out in the worst way, and here I was getting involved with every woman's wet dream. They came on to him every second of the day. How could I trust that he wouldn't fuck another bitch the moment I turned my head? That was a lot to ask a girl from the country with three girls and a teenage sister to raise.

I was about to answer him, but we had pulled up in front of Jason's club. The paparazzi was on a thousand as we stepped out of the car. Kente made sure to rush to my side the moment his feet hit the pavement and the valet helped me out the car. The paparazzi asked so many fucking questions with cameras flashing every which way. It was overwhelming and I didn't know if I was built for this kind of life. I still didn't know how Felicity managed to keep her cool all this time.

"'Bout time you showed up. Kente, you gone be late to the second coming, huh?" Felicity joked. She complimented me on my outfit and then handed me a shot of Patrón.

"Thanks, boo. How do you deal with that shit out there? I don't know if I'm ready for all that," I admitted.

"Aw, boo. Don't let that run you away from something that could be great for you. Trust me. I think you should do the show. And put a gag order on Devante and his pet," she said.

"Y'all just won't stop until I say yes. Okay, I give up. I'll do it," I relented.

Kente must've been ear hustling because he scooped me up and put me on his lap. He then put a mean kiss on me that had me ready to nut on myself right then and there. I forgot I was in a club for a minute and returned the kiss by sliding my tongue in his mouth. We were completely caught up in each other. I had never had this feeling about any man before, not even Devante.

"Damn," we said at the same time when we broke our kiss finally. I looked over my shoulder and everyone was staring at us.

"Uh-uh. Y'all need to stop. Ain't no love in the club tonight," Megan joked.

She jumped up when she heard "Sex Talk" by Megan Thee Stallion come on. She started to dip and twerk her ass so good, I knew she could have made some real money in the strip club. When I saw how Kwame was looking at his wife, I knew he was about to try and knock her ass right back up later.

I jumped up with her and started shaking my ass right along with her. Felicity was playing it cool, but sexy. She was grinding on Jason's lap and I knew that his dick was probably hard under her. I wouldn't put it past them to sneak off and get a quickie in. It wouldn't be the first time that they left me in the club to do their thing and come back.

We enjoyed our night and us ladies got drunk as hell. It felt good to get out without my girls and have some adult fun. It felt even better to have the attention of a man that could have any woman he wanted with just a wink. But he made it clear to anyone that had a working ear he was interested in just me. I felt so good when I laid my head on my pillow after Kente dropped me off.

My phone going off woke me up out of a peaceful sleep. Irritated, I sat up in my bed and looked down at the screen. I rolled my eyes when I saw Devante's number flashing on the screen. I huffed and picked up my phone prepared to hear whatever it was that he had to say.

"I see you're out being a hoe instead of a mother. Where the fuck are my kids?" he asked. I counted to ten in my head before I answered him.

"First, that animal you lay with every night is a hoe. I went out with friends last night. Don't be mad now that I upgraded in a major way. Your daughters are fine, and you would know that if you would call or come and see them. But you got your son and it was just fuck us, huh?" I was getting heated and I hated that he managed to get under my skin like he did.

"I told you that I'm coming. Damn, you can't cut a nigga some slack," he said. He repeated the same line whenever he would call, and I was over it.

"Look, it's early and I still have to get the girls' hair done. Do you want to pick them up and take them for the day?" I asked, trying to once again open the door for him to be a father.

"I can't today. You need to give me time. You can't just ask me to take the girls at the last minute," he huffed.

"Whatever. I knew you weren't. I was just hoping for once that you would prove me wrong," I said.

"I don't know why you tripping. I said just let me know ahead of time. Shit, you get some new dick and you start acting brand new. I don't even know why I fucked with your ass," he ranted.

"Really, nigga? You gone sit on this phone after I put up with your shit since senior year? Fighting bitches left and right, three STDs, three daughters and I left my home to be with you. I did all of that and you still left me for a bitch that could double as Yogi Bear! Don't you even fix your lips to say I'm acting brand new!

"You mad? Your ass should be. That nigga has bank, and he actually listens to what I have to say. I didn't even look in his direction. I was still hung up on your ass until recently. He pursued me and is still pursuing me. You wouldn't know a thing about putting me and your daughters first. I just pray that you treat her better than you did me," I said and hung up the phone.

I was drained from that phone call and I just wanted to lay right back down, but I knew that I would be in the salon all day with the girls. So, I got up and took a quick shower and threw on a pair of cotton shorts and a matching top. I slid my feet into a pair of Fenty slides and headed out to the kitchen to fix breakfast for the girls.

"Damn, who pissed on you this morning?" Francesca asked me when I walked in the kitchen.

"Who else?" I muttered. I grabbed a bag of grits out of the pantry, eggs, butter, cream, cheese and bacon out of the refrigerator. I put the items on the counter and grabbed pots, pans and seasonings out of the cabinets, I proceeded to fix bacon, omelets and cheese grits. After I fixed the food and piled them on serving trays, the girls dug into their food.

"You guys hurry up and eat so we can go and see Michaela," I told the girls just as my doorbell rang.

"Who are all those people?" Francesca asked me while she was looking out of the window.

I went to the door and opened it to find Kente standing there with a whole glam squad. A wide grin spread across my face when I saw him holding a huge vase of Gerbera daisies in his hands. I stepped back and let him and the women in the house before speaking.

"What is all of this?" I asked him and gave him a quick peck on the cheek.

"You said that you had to get the girls' hair done and that it takes forever. So, I had my friends here come over and help get the girls together. Then we can take all of you shopping. Francesca, I think you need to get some new shit. This is your senior year and you're doing double duty with the nursing classes. You deserve to be treated," Kente said.

Francesca jumped up and down and the ran into Kente's arms, giving him a big hug. She rushed out of the room to find her some clothes to wear out to the mall, and all I could do was laugh. I did my best to provide for my sister, and my parents did send money for her to get her some things. But what Kente was doing said so much about his character that I was immediately smitten.

"You know you don't have to do all of this," I said while the women set up in my kitchen.

"I know I don't have to, but I want to. You work hard as hell to take care of your daughters and now you have your sister. This is just to show you how much I admire you. Now you need to go with Rhea and let her hook you up with some clothes. I smell cheese grits," he said, and speed walked to the pots on the stove.

"Wait, come again," I said and slapped his hand away from the pots. "Care to explain Rhea and me picking out a wardrobe," I demanded.

"I mean, you really didn't think that I would do all of this for the girls and not let you in on all of the fun," he told me.

"I don't know what I did to deserve this," I said with a blush coloring my face.

"Just by being you. I told you that you will be mine and I am determined to make that happen soon. I don't do that friend zone shit well," he admitted.

I smiled and fixed him a plate before heading to my room where Rhea had a bunch of clothes laid out on my bed. I saw this green and black Fendi sundress that I had fallen in love with on the website. I wanted it, but the price tag on it forced me to go to Fashion Nova and see if they had one similar on their website. I loved fashion, but not enough to end up homeless over it.

"I see you looking at that dress. Kente paid for everything already, so you can keep it all if you want to. He said that you were worth this and more. I don't know what you did to him, but you got my cousin sprung!" she exclaimed.

"Your cousin?" I asked.

"Girl, yes. He and his brother paid for me to go to college and get my degrees in business and fashion. I always wanted to be a stylist because I love to shop. So, when Kente made it when we were teenagers, he promised that he would help pay for school. And now look at me. The personal stylist to one of the hottest labels out there," she explained.

That made me fall for Kente a little bit more. The things that I was finding out about that man had me feeling weak in the knees. Instead of responding to Rhea, I went into my bathroom and slid my body into the dress. It fit me like a glove and felt like heaven on my skin.

I walked back out and put on a pair of matching Fendi sandals and pulled my hair out the usual ponytail I kept it in. I decided to let my raven hair fall down my back for once. I sprayed on my Armani perfume and slid some clear gloss on my lips. Rhea had hung up all the clothes in my closet and I didn't protest this time. I was going to talk to Kente about buying me expensive items all the time.

While I loved it, I wasn't to be bought. One simple flower, or a phone call just to say hi was enough to make my heart skip a beat or two. I didn't want much from a man. Just loyalty and commitment to only me. I didn't want to be lied to about anything. I was a very honest person, even if it meant that I would be the one hurt in the end, but that was just me. I kept it ninety-eight plus two at all times. I just wanted the same in return.

Raven

This bitch was really getting on my nerves. I was tired of seeing her name in the blogs and all over billboards in Atlanta. Felicity was a name and face that I wanted to be a distant memory. Two men that I once had control over basically left my ass for dead. They hadn't tried to reach out or even see if I was still alive. Both of them claimed that they loved me, but where was that love when my father dragged me out of my home and sold it?

I was starting to get used to living in Ramon's compound, though. There was the main house that we lived in, four guest houses, then three small homes for the staff that chose to live on the grounds. There was a stable with five horses, a small golf course, two basketball courts, and I swear I saw a helipad. It was like a palace and I was the reigning queen of the land.

"You look like you're enjoying yourself," Ramon said as he came out of the shower.

I still hadn't let him touch me, but Lord knows that man was fine. I needed dick like yesterday, and it was hard to resist this nigga. The way his abs were glistening with the water from the shower had me soaking the sheets that I was laying on.

"I was, but then you decided to walk in here," I spat. I had to do something to keep my growing attraction at bay.

"I know you want me. You can quit with all of the anger and verbal jabs. Now go get dressed. You need to make yourself known again," he said and dropped his towel.

The sight of that man's ass that seemed as if God himself sculpted it… I watched as the muscles in his back rippled while he stepped into his boxer briefs. He smoothed his hair back on his head and I wanted to take a bite out of him. I shook my head and climbed out of the bed. I went straight into the bathroom to take a shower.

I turned the water on as hot as I could stand it and then hit the steam function on the shower button. I hooked my phone up to the sound bar in the bathroom and started playing Saweetie. I wanted to feel better about my situation and Saweetie was a whole mood. I turned up the music and started to rap along with her while dancing naked.

"A rich nigga, eight figure that's my type! Aye!" I yelled while bouncing my ass.

"Oh, really. So, I'm your type?" I heard Ramon say. I whipped my body around, instantly angry.

"Can I have a little privacy? I mean damn, can a bitch take a shower without you on my ass?" I yelled and shut off my music.

"This is my house and I will enter whatever room I feel like it. You can go and shower. I'll see you at the breakfast table," he said and left me alone.

I showered quickly and finished up my morning hygiene. After I finished in the bathroom, I went and put on a Dolce & Gabbana maxi dress and left my pedicured feet bare. I plodded down the hall and took the elevator down to the conservatory for breakfast. We had breakfast here every morning for some dumb ass reason.

Since I detoxed, I was seeing things very clearly. I still hated Felicity and I knew that I wanted her gone and out of the picture permanently. Even though I didn't want to be romantically linked to Ramon, I figured that I could use his power and influence to help me achieve my goal.

"Breakfast looks good this morning," I said sweetly.

The table was full of fruit, pastries, bagels, sausage, eggs and bacon. There was softened butter, cream cheese, marmalade and juice as well as fresh coffee. I was starving and went right to the food. I didn't even speak to Ramon because my stomach was having a more important conversation. Ramon sat back, drank his coffee and smirked while I devoured my food.

"What's with the bipolar behavior? Upstairs you're cussing me out and now you're smiling and being polite. Tell me what it is that you want," he stated.

"Honestly, I want revenge. I want to get rid of the woman that has my life. She has these men running behind her young ass like she's the best thing since lace fronts. I can't have that shit," I honestly said.

"Don't you think you need to let that go? I mean, obviously you're doing better than her. Look at where you're living. You have more money than you can ever spend. You have custom made clothes from exclusive designers. You have servants, a fleet of cars and expense accounts in stores all over the world. Why would you even stoop down and become a basic bitch?" he asked me.

"Because I lost my freedom because of that bitch. She walked in and then my life fell apart. She has to go. It was because of her that Jason cut me off and treated me like shit!" I roared.

I slammed my fist on the table and a platter of croissants fell and broke on the ground. I knew to the average person that I sounded cray, but I felt justified in my reasoning. I just needed Ramon to help me out because he was well connected, and he could get me what I needed.

"You lost that on your own. That was your own damn fault. Imagine how well off you would be had you got with me when you had the chance. Shit, you have the chance now, but you're still stuck up under that fuckboy," he spat with jealousy tinging his voice.

"Well, if Jason was suffering, then I would be more open to you," I reasoned, trying to butter him up.

"I don't like what you're trying to do, but I can never refuse you anything. But you have to do something for me," he said.

"What's that?" I asked nervously.

"Marry me in the next month. You can plan the wedding of the century. There is no budget. You marry me and I will make sure that you can have the revenge you want so badly," he said.

The thought of ridding the world of that self-serving bitch Felicity was enough for me. I didn't love Ramon by a longshot, but the fact that he was going to help me kill this bitch was enough for me. I would have married Flavor Flav if he promised me the same shit.

"I'll do it. I'll marry you!" I exclaimed happily.

Even though it was for reasons other than marriage, it seemed to please Ramon. He got up from his chair and walked over to where I was sitting. He pulled me up from my seat and cradled me in his arms bridal style. He walked toward the elevator, carrying me the entire way. When the doors opened, he walked us in and hit the button to our level with his elbow.

The doors had barely closed before he devoured my lips with his. Sparks went off from the top of my head to my feet. Good Lord, that man could kiss. His lips were as soft as cocoa butter and I could taste the coffee and fruit that he had for breakfast on his breath. His large hands were gripping my ass as he changed how he was holding me. I had my legs wrapped around him and I knew he could feel the heat from my pussy on his stomach.

I felt the cool air on my back when the elevator doors opened, and Ramon took me to our suite of rooms. He gently laid me down on the bed and just stared at me lustfully. I looked up at him, and for the first time, I really looked at him and liked what I saw. I pulled my dress over my head and exposed my naked frame.

"You're so beautiful," he said, and then he lifted my legs up and spread them apart.

I didn't get a chance to respond because he had started to kiss my southern lips gently for a moment. Once he got a taste of how sweet my nectar was, he went nuts. He nibbled on my pearl and lapped up my juices like it was the last thing he would ever drink. I couldn't form a single word because he had taken my ability to speak just that fast.

Three quick licks later, my nut was squirting all over his face and neck. When I came down from that ride, I opened my eyes and Ramon was standing before me naked as the day he was born. And damn! He was built even better in the front. His chiseled, rock hard abs looked like you could wash clothes on them. His light brown skin was smooth, hair and tattoo free. You could tell that he spent a lot of time in the gym on the property.

And that dick. Whew! That thing was eleven inches of pure steel. It was long, thick and veiny like I liked them. It had a slight curve going to the left that I knew was about to have my ass climbing the walls if his dick game was anything like his tongue game. It had been so long since I got some good dick that even mediocre dick would do for now.

"Shit!" I cried out when he penetrated me. He was stretching me out in ways that I hadn't been stretched before.

He was giving me long, deep strokes, and I swear I felt his dick shifting my liver. He was hitting spots that I never knew I had and the whole time I was thinking about Jason and how he used to fuck me into a coma. The thoughts of Jason and the feel of Ramon's curved dick sent my body into overdrive. I let off back-to-back orgasms that lifted my body off the bed. Not long after my endless nut, Ramon came hard and filled my entire core up with his babies.

I wasn't worried about getting pregnant because I was sure that my IUD was still intact. I just shifted on the bed and slid off into a blissful, sex-filled nap knowing that my dreams of revenge and anger were about to come true.

Dylan

I couldn't believe my plan failed. But I should have known better. That one kiss wasn't enough to break Jason and Fefe up, but I was sure that I had planted seeds of doubt all up and through Jason's mind. He came across as this arrogant asshole, but I knew the truth. He was just as human as the rest of us. And his old ass couldn't handle a young thing like Fefe.

I explored her virgin walls first and I would be the last, if I had anything to say about it. I was sitting in my condo sipping on a cup of lean and it was barely past eight in the morning. I was supposed to meet up with Kente in the studio, but I was cool on his ass. He was supposed to be helping get my girl back, but he was too busy trying to get in her friend's pussy to even do me a favor, so fuck him.

"My goodness, Dylan, you really need to hire someone to clean this mess up," I heard my mother say.

"Son, we're worried about you. All of this drinking, the DUI, trying to come in between Fefe's relationship. That's not the son we raised. We don't recognize this Dylan," my father said.

I was sitting in my home listening to my folks since they wanted to have a "family chat." All this shit was, was an intervention. They were trying to get my ass into rehab and that wasn't going to happen. At least not until I got Felicity to go on a date with me. Then I might think about it.

"Like y'all give a shit. All you two care about is if I can still pay your fucking mortgages and shit. Y'all never gave a fuck about me. If y'all did, then you would have let me and my baby momma stay together!" I roared.

"I did what I thought was best. Your father spoiled you too much. Why would I let my son ruin his life that way? And with a black bitch at that! I would be laughed out of my country club," my mom admitted.

I looked at my dad with his head hanging and I knew there was some shit that they weren't telling me. I knew that my mom had to be the one that made it impossible for me to be there for my family, but the way my dad was just sitting there, let me know that there was so much more that they weren't saying.

"Oh, because your racist ass friends wouldn't speak to you, you denied your granddaughter!" I yelled.

"I denied her ass because she will never be my grandchild! That bastard will never be able to call me anything but ma'am. I do not want a black child sitting at my dining room table. You're just like your father. You both like dark meat," she spat.

"What the fuck is she talking about, Dad?" I asked.

"Oh, he won't tell you. I will, though. You know that we're divorced, but you don't know the reason why. He left me for that black whore that handled your career," she explained.

"You mean Della? I mean, what would you think would happen, Mom? I mean, she was more than my manager. She was around when you weren't. Hell, she and Dad were the ones that raised me. You spent your time at the spa and getting your body stitched up so tight that if you bend the right way, you might bust at the seams! Hell, I wish he would have left your ass a long time ago. Then I would have my family and career," I ranted.

My mom's face was so red, she looked like a weathered tomato. I finally spoke my truth straight from my heart. I let her know how I felt that she was the one that ruined my life. I told her that I hated her and that I never wanted to see her again. She could tell her little friends that she no longer had a son, so that she could ignore the fact that she was indeed a forty-seven year-old grandmother.

"You, you don't mean that Dylan. What am I supposed to do without you?" she cried.

"You mean what are you going to do without my money. Tell you what, I'll put a million in your account today and then you're on your own." I turned back to my father and didn't say a word until I heard her heels fading and my door closing.

"So, you and Della?" I asked my dad.

"Yes, son. She's a wonderful woman. I tried to fight my feelings for her, but we had been around each other every single day since you were about four. Somehow, we just went from making sure you were at auditions, to a lunch here and there, and then we were in love. We're getting married in six months, and we want you there. But you have to be clean, sober and over your obsession with Felicity. You just need to be a father to your child and not worry about what goes on in the mother's life," my father advised.

"I'll try and do better," I said just to shut his ass up.

My dad stood up, patted me on my shoulder and then left me alone with my thoughts. I fixed my third cup of lean for the morning and sat back on my sofa. I fixed some eggs and toast so that I could actually put some food in my stomach and turned on the television. I regretted it as soon as I saw the program that was on.

Revolt, Diddy's channel, was playing The Breakfast Club, and Angela Yee's rumor report was on. Big and bold was a picture of Jason and Felicity looking into each other's eyes. They were at an event for Cîroc vodka, and Felicity was the new spokeswoman for the brand. Angela Yee's voice made my skin crawl while she basically fawned all over my baby momma and her man.

"Last night at the launch of the new Mixed Berry Cîroc, singer and actress Fefe Brooks made her debut as the new spokeswoman for the brand. She and her boo Jason Miller looked like they were completely in love, and that incident with her baby daddy seemed like a thing of the past. If they keep looking at each other like that, we may be seeing a baby or wedding in the near future," she said.

"Like hell! That will never happen as long as I'm alive!" I yelled at the television. I picked up the glass of whiskey that my father was drinking and hurled it at the screen. My television cracked and then it went black along with my heart.

If I couldn't have Felicity, then nobody would.

Jason

"I think you should take the part. I mean, you were the first choice anyway. Now that Julie dropped out because of her pregnancy, this is the perfect opportunity for you. *Post Wives* won't work without you. Plus, you can be an executive producer on the show."

I was lounging around my house with Felicity and Avalon trying to convince my lady to take the role that brought her into my life. She was a little hesitant because she thought that it would take away from her studio time and time with Avalon. I was trying to reassure her that she would have time for both because I would clear her schedule for it. I was the boss, as a matter of fact.

"I don't know, babe, it just seems like there won't be enough time to do this," she complained as she leaned on my chest.

"Look, Daniel makes the shooting schedule and he won't shoot for more than eight hours a day. He does believe in having a life outside of the studio. Especially with all of the kids he has," I explained to her.

"How long do I have to decide?" she asked, and then I knew I had her.

"Three days. We start shooting next week. And by then, we can get into a routine with Avalon and school," I told her.

She looked up at me with those big, beautiful eyes and I couldn't resist her. I leaned down and placed my lips on hers and gave her a sweet kiss. She leaned up to deepen the kiss and snaked her tongue in my mouth. No matter how many times this woman kissed me, it always felt like it was the first time.

"Keep this up and Avalon gone be a big sister," I murmured on her lips. Felicity smiled at me and started to unbuckle my pants.

"Hey, Jason, can Ione and Juliette come over? Clark went over her friend's house and I'm bored watching you and Mommy kiss all the time," Avalon asked, breaking up what was sure to be an intense fuck session.

"It's fine by me. But you have to ask their mom and your mom," I told her.

"Let me call Ginger and see if she's okay with it. We can order pizza and play some games," Felicity said over her shoulder while dialing Ginger's number.

An hour later, Ginger was sitting in my kitchen while Felicity was fixing a huge bowl of popcorn for the girls. I knew that Ginger had to be bored if she was hanging in the house with us on her night off from work. Kente was in the studio and probably would be for a few more hours. I told her that she was more than welcome to hang out with us until the girls fell asleep, and she took me up on that offer.

"So, when do you start filming?" I asked her.

"In two weeks. I'm so nervous. I've never done anything like this before. Am I really ready to have everybody all up in my business like that?" she questioned.

"Chile, they already up in your business. They stay posting about you and Kente. Y'all are relationship goals for me," Felicity said, and I looked at her like I was hurt.

"Oh, word. That's how we doing it now?" I asked.

"Aw, you are my man crush every day, but you know it took you a minute to get the hang of how to woo me," she joked.

I just laughed because that was Felicity. She always knew how to make me feel like I was doing everything right. She let me know when I was messing up and kept my head in the game. She was the one that told me when I was spending too much time under her and neglecting business. She was definitely my other half. I was going to put a ring on it soon. I just needed to get everyone involved that loved her.

"I don't know what she's talking about, but you two are my relationship goals," Ginger said while drinking her glass of wine.

"At least I have one person in my corner," I joked back.

"Awwwww, he's mad. I'm sorry, baby," Felicity said. She came over and gave me a quick peck on the lips, leaving her lip gloss all over me.

"You and that damn lip gloss," I said, wiping my mouth off with a paper towel.

"Boy, please. My lip gloss be poppin'," she said.

We all broke out laughing at Felicity's silliness. I sat back and listened to the two of them talk about hair, makeup and wardrobe for the show. I was already on it for her. I told Rhea to make sure that she gave Ginger a closet full of designer gear. She had a hair and makeup team on standby to make sure that she always looked her best when she was out on the scene. Ginger was another star in the making and I was happy that I would have a hand in it.

"I still can't believe that I'm about to be on TV! And *Love and Hip Hop* for fucks sake! This is so crazy!" Ginger exclaimed.

"So, what does Devante have to say about all of this?" Felicity asked.

"Oh, his bitch ass was going on and on about how I was a gold-digging hoe and that he was going to take the girls from me. You know, typical ass-hurt, fuck boy shit," she said dismissively.

"You know we can get a gag order put on him. Just say the word," I told her.

I meant that shit, too. I was sick and tired of these niggas thinking they could make babies and leave them for the mother to raise. My dad was heavy in the streets, but he took care of me and my brother. He never let my mom do it on her own. Even when Jasiel died from leukemia, my dad was right there.

That's why I was willing to go above and beyond for Felicity and Ginger. They were given the short end of the stick when it came down to the men that fathered their children, and that wasn't their fault. Devante had another thing coming if he thought that he would try and use Ginger making money as a way to hurt her or her daughters. She was like a sister to me now, and my nieces deserved better.

"It's cool. Because I plan on being completely honest with the world about my situation. I still plan on working at least part-time. You never know how things will work out. I need to keep a back-up plan," Ginger said.

"Trust me, you won't need that job with my team behind you. By this time next year, you will be a household name." Ginger's eyes lit up and I knew that this was going to be a good move on all our parts.

Felicity

"You have two interviews this week. One with Dish Nation and then you have the Lip Service podcast. Then you have two appearances at the OLG restaurant and The Pink Teacup," Anita, my new assistant, explained to me as she ran down my week.

We were halfway done with filming *Post Wives* for the fall season and I was loving it. Filming was moving so smoothly, even with all of the bloopers. Daniel made sure we stuck to his schedule. We had to have makeup and wardrobe done and be on set within two hours of arriving. He had the schedule down to a science, and we were moving like a well-oiled machine.

I was also putting on the finishing touches of my album. My first single, "Love's Breakdown," was set to be released soon. My dreams were coming true and it was exhausting. I felt like I was being pulled in fifty different directions, and when I got home at night, it was all I could do to make it to my bed. Thank goodness Jason and Avalon were so understanding.

"Damn, baby. You over here looking all good and shit in that dress. Make a nigga want to do some things," Jason said and wrapped his arms around my waist from behind.

"Chill, you know my man owns this company. I told you to meet me in my trailer," I joked as I leaned into his signature fragrance of Creed.

"Man, don't get fucked up. This not no Eddie Cibrian and LeAnn Rimes shit," he said, referring to when we watched one of my favorite Lifetime movies. I told him how they got together on the set of the movie and he almost pulled me off the project.

"Damn, it's so easy to get a rise out of you," I joked.

"Keep on and watch you get replaced," he mumbled and stormed off.

I don't know who pissed in his Corn Flakes this morning, but he better learn how to put sugar on them shits and keep it moving. Ever since that kiss with Dylan months ago, he had been acting jealous and insecure. I thought that we had moved past it, but I guess not. I mean, Dylan was slowly working his way into Avalon's life, so I figured that must be what it was. I went over to my trailer where I knew he was heading over to change and talk to him.

"What's wrong? I was only joking out there," I asked him when I walked in the trailer.

Jason was busy in his phone, texting furiously. Whatever he was mad at, he was taking it out on that poor iPhone. I didn't even think he heard me when I came in and started talking, because the conversation he was having was so intense at the moment.

"Sorry, sweetheart. I had to handle something. But I want to know why this man keeps on posting you as his Woman Crush Wednesday. And then this," he said and held his phone up to my face when I sat down across from him.

There was a picture on Dylan's Instagram with him and Avalon at my house. they were standing in the front yard hugging and smiling. I remember that picture because he was dropping my daughter off and Ione was outside with her mom. Ione took the picture and then the girls and Ginger came in the house with me and chilled out. But his caption made it seem like more than it was.

Getting my family back. Nothing like a daughter's love.

"Okay, first of all, you know damn well I told you about that picture. I wasn't anywhere near them. I was in MY house minding my got damn business. I don't even speak to Dylan when he decides to pick up Avalon. You know he's her father and he is doing well enough now that he can hang out with her for a few hours on the weekend. I thought that we discussed this already," I sighed.

"Yeah, okay. That better be all it is," he said.

"Look, I'm not about to argue with you over this. You knew what I had going on months ago and you still chose to be with me. Jason, I love you and only you. You are literally the first man that I have ever loved or been in a relationship with. After Avalon, I stayed away from boys until I enlisted. Then the trifling shit they did made me stay further away. You have to stop thinking about the next nigga taking me from you and think about how that shit will drive me to him. Jealousy is not a good look or a healthy meal for a relationship," I explained.

"Damn! Why the fuck you got to be so mature about everything? That shit is sexy as fuck. I'm not even mad at you. I just worry that our ages will get in the way sometimes. Like maybe you might want someone closer to your own age that you have more in common with," he admitted.

"Now, that's crazy. What in the hell would I have in common with those niggas? None of them have been through what I've been through. And all they want to do is sip lean and fuck off on random ass bitches. You got me from day one and that hasn't changed. Stop letting Dylan get to you, baby," I said.

I walked over to my trailer door and locked it. We had almost another hour before we started to shoot the next scene, so I was about to make the best of my time. I pulled off the dress I was wearing and exposed the pink bra and panty set that I had chosen to wear that morning. I walked back over in front of Jason and let him get an eyeful of me.

"Just beautiful," he gasped and took a handful of my ass.

I threw my head back and let out a moan of pleasure while he kneaded my ass like he was making bread. He pulled me closer to him and traced his lips around my belly button. His warm tongue worked its way up towards my breasts where he had unfastened my bra in one quick motion. He looked up at me, licked his lips and started sucking on my left breast like he was a baby trying to get his meal.

He slid his long fingers into the side of my panties, making their way into my warm core. He started stirring my juices like he was making his own sweet tea. I moaned low and long as his fingers continued their sexual stirring. My body began to heat up and a small sheen of sweat formed on my body. I was close to my peak, but Jason had other plans.

He gently moved me out of the way and stripped out of the khaki slacks and polo-style shirt. His dick was straining against the compression shorts that I made him wear. Even with those on, his print was still impressive. My mouth started watering at the sight of his body. I wasn't as experienced as most of the women that Jason had been with, but that made having sex with him that much more intense. He was able to teach me what he liked and how he liked it. He had turned me into a complete freak, and I loved how free he made me feel.

Jason turned me around and walked me towards my makeup table. He bent me over the vanity and ripped my panties off. There went that set. It was the tenth set that he had ruined that way. It didn't matter because he made sure that I had plenty of underwear. Once again, he started to knead my ass before giving it a hard smack. I moaned in pleasure and my juices began leaking down my leg. Jason bent down and started to lick my juices all the way up until his lips met my southern lips and gave them a deep, but quick kiss.

He came back up, spread my cheeks and slowly entered me from behind. No matter how many times we made love, I still had to get used to his size. He gave me long, deep strokes, managing to hit my g-spot every single time. I squeezed my muscles tight around him and began to throw my ass back on him making him go crazy. He began to speed up his thrusts and bang my back out.

"Fuck! Right there, daddy. Shit! Just like that!" I whispered loudly.

"This my shit! Don't ever give it away, you hear me?" he demanded as he pounded his flesh into my flesh.

"I promise, daddy! Fuck, I'm about to cum!" I cried out as I felt my pussy tingle, and my sweet nectar flowed out of me and all over his dick.

He grunted and went ape shit. He gripped my waist tight and began to thrust in and out of me like he never did before. He was trying to write his name in my soul with his dick. I was well on my way to a second orgasm and exploded just as he sent his babies deep into my womb. I was sure that he had gotten my ass pregnant by the nut he busted.

"I think we made a baby," he said, panting as we tried to regain our composure.

"Probably," I laughed. I walked to the other end of the trailer where my shower was to wash up quickly.

Jason got dressed and lit my scented candles to erase the smells of our love making. My hair and makeup team were about to show up to fix me up for the next scene where I was supposed to be beaten up. I had to be fresh and ready to go by the time they got there, and I didn't want them all up in my business. Even though they were cool, I didn't share my personal life with anyone on set. We were coworkers at this point. I was friendly with my on-screen best friend, but we weren't close.

"I'm ready to bend that ass over again," Jason said when I came out of my shower wrapped in a fluffy robe. My hair was laying down in soft curls and I smelled like Herbal Essence shampoo.

"Boy, bye!" I said. He had just grabbed me and kissed me when Jackie and Janet came in for hair and makeup.

"We can come back," Jackie's ass had the nerve to joke. She was always making jokes about me and Jason.

"I'm just going to go before they make me fire them," Jason joked. He was in a better mood now that he got a shot of lunchtime pussy.

"Okay, baby. Can you pick up Avalon from Ginger's? She's supposed to be filming today and I don't want Avalon near the shit that's about to go on in that house," I told him.

He agreed and kissed me before he left. My girl was doing her thing with the show. I had filmed a couple of scenes with her when the show asked me. They wanted me to join, but I told them that I would only shoot one or two scenes with my girl. I would not become a cast member. I had too much going on to deal with Mona Scott and the shenanigans that went on with her shows. But my girl was looking like she was going to become a fan favorite on the upcoming season.

It only took thirty minutes to get hair and makeup done and then I was back on set for another four hours. By the time we finished shooting the last few scenes of that episode, I was mentally exhausted. My character, Zoe, had been beaten and raped and it took me back to when my father tried to take advantage of me. It was easy for me to get into character because I used my own pain to make the scenes more believable. But it made me wish that I never showed up for work that day.

"Fefe, you are amazing! I don't know what or how you do it, but you make shooting so easy. We only had to do three takes today. At this rate we'll be done for the spring lineup earlier than expected," Daniel praised me as we wrapped.

"I just thought about something from my past. That's all," I said. I was ready to go, and I was hoping that Jason's cousin would take the hint.

"Well, I won't keep you. See you tomorrow!" he said and walked off with one of the directors.

I headed towards my trailer to get back in my street clothes. All I wanted was a mushroom and black olive pizza with some ginger ale to eat. Then a foot rub and maybe some dick to end the night would make my mood shift. But I saw that I wasn't about to get any peace when I saw Dorinda's ass waiting for me outside of my trailer.

"Can we talk?" she asked.

"Why should I talk to you?" I asked.

"I just want to see my grandchild. You owe me that much," she demanded.

"Just like you owe me for all the years of back child support that you made sure that Dylan couldn't pay me. You made sure that you lived well while your granddaughter struggled because her mom was a kid herself and couldn't get a job. You had me blacklisted and I couldn't book a job if I paid someone off. So, you can't demand shit from me," I stated.

"I will take your little ass to court. See how they will like it when I tell the judge about your former drug dealer boyfriend," she threatened.

"And then all of your pasty-faced country club friends will find out that your son fucked the young ass black bitch and had a kid with her. How will that make you look? Your son likes black pussy and so does your husband. Try me, you racist bitch!" I screamed.

"All I want is to see her, please! I don't have anyone left. I'm sorry for everything. I was wrong, and I lost my family because of it. Just please, let me make it right," she pleaded.

I softened when I saw the genuinely sincere look in her eyes. This was a woman that lost it all and had hit rock bottom. It was all over the blogs how Dylan cut her out of his life, and she was now on her own. She had been completely humbled and only came at me because she was scared. I knew how it felt when you're backed in a corner and the world seems to be coming for you.

"Give me your number and I'll let you know if Avalon is up for it. I can't promise you that she will be open to it, but I will try my best. It's time for you to change your ways, Dorinda. Black people are not bad people," I advised her.

"Thank you. I know that. I was raised to think that way, but looking at you and how you beat the odds has told me so much. I know you're a good person and I know my granddaughter is in great hands with you." She came over to me and pulled me into a hug.

I almost pushed her off of me in a reflex, but my arms automatically circled around her. I felt her tears soaking me through my shirt, and it made me pull her tighter. I whispered that things will be okay, and that God wouldn't give us more than we could handle.

She let go, looked at me and smiled before leaving me alone. I felt a whole world lighter after that conversation. I just hoped that Avalon's father would get it together as fast as his mother did.

Ginger

When I tell you that filming for this show was hard, shit was harder than translating Chinese to Greek. I had already seen three fights and thrown a drink on a bird ass bitch that didn't know how to stay out of my business. Now here I was sitting in my living room with Devante so we could "talk."

"All I'm saying is that you need to check your bitch. She has one more time to disrespect my kids and I'm going to put my foot in her ass," I warned.

"You straight wilding for no fucking reason. All I'm saying is that you got to cut a nigga some slack," he pleaded.

"The fuck you mean, my nigga? You really think I trust your ass after the way you left us for dead for that Ursula looking bitch and your son? What, we weren't good enough for you? You know what, unless you want to see your girls, we don't need to talk," I stated, and stood up to let him know that he needed to leave my house.

"You right about that. At least that Ursula looking bitch not out here fucking for a come up. You out here being a hoe around my girls. At least my bitch got some sense! Dumb ass hoe," Devante spat at me.

Baby, when I tell you I went off, I went Lynn Whitfield in *A Thin Line Between Love and Hate*. I cussed him six ways to Sunday and then threw a vase of blue roses that Kente gave me at his head. All of this was being recorded for *Love and Hip Hop*. They were going to have a field day with this shit. I spoke rapidly in English and Spanish, cursing Devante, his mama, his mama's mama and his raggedy ass daddy that helped make his sorry ass.

I was so mad that I forgot the cameras were even there. I didn't even notice that Kente had walked in the house. He walked into the middle of World War III and couldn't do anything at first. But when he heard me snapping about Devante calling me out my name, he went into attack mode. He laid Devante out in one punch. I didn't know that Kente had it in him.

"We need to wrap this up and get this man out of here. Kente, can you go in the kitchen while we get him out of here? I think we're finished here. I'm so sorry about all of this," one of the show's producers said to me.

I didn't say anything to him because this sit down was his idea. I just walked into the kitchen to talk to Kente who was pacing back and forth. His dark face was even darker, and his hair had fallen from his normal man bun and was hanging wildly around his face. His anger was so sexy to me. This man didn't ask any questions, he just jumped right to my defense and I felt like it was finally time to give this man some pussy.

It had been four months since we had been seeing each other and we had been celibate. I was very particular about who I gave my goods to and I hadn't slept with anyone since Devante and I broke up. I used to tease Felicity about her coochie cobwebs, but my shit was dried up like prunes.

"You okay, love?" he asked when he saw me.

"I should be asking you that. I mean, you laid his ass out with the quickness. I just want you to know what went on," I started, then told him all about our conversation.

"He's lucky all I did was knock his ass out. He really don't know me to

48

be speaking on my ass. And you are so far from a hoe, you almost a got damn nun," he joked.

"Word. Well, nun this," I said and slid out of my pants.

I tossed them in his direction and walked off towards my room. I heard him mumble something and then his heavy footsteps followed behind me. By the time he got to my room, I was already undressed in nothing but a thong. My titties were sitting up nicely on my chest despite having nursed three children. My stomach was still flat due to my daily yoga routine. My hips were slim, but my ass showed my black side. Being half-Mexican and half-black made it hard for me to fit in back home, but here in Atlanta, I was a hot commodity for my exotic look.

"Shit, I need to knock niggas out more often," Kente said, standing in the doorway.

He walked in the room and closed the door. Before I could react, he had my body pinned under him and he had covered my mouth with his. I knew he could feel the heat rising from my southern lips as he kissed my worries away. He parted my lips with his tongue and mine reached forward to dance with his. His hands roamed my body while we shared a passionate kiss.

I pulled back from the kiss long enough to pull Kente's shirt over his head. I loved his chocolate skin and the way it covered his body. He wasn't built like a body builder, but his stocky build was something that I was always attracted to. I didn't like a lot of muscles and Kente had just the right amount.

I gathered up my strength and flipped Kente onto his back. I unbuckled his Tom Ford jeans and set him free. Damn, I knew the Bintu men had to be blessed, but this nigga had a whole horse between his legs. He had to be at least ten inches and he wasn't even all the way hard yet. I was about to be walking funny for the next few weeks for sure. But for now, I was about to lay back and enjoy this pipe down.

· · ·

THE NEXT MORNING, I was up early fixing breakfast while Kente was asleep in my bed. He'd sent my body on an orgasmic high that I had never experienced before. My pussy was still throbbing from where his dick spent the night stroking me. My hair was still tangled and all over my head, but I didn't care. He deserved this breakfast to be brought to him and he needed to see what I looked like in the morning if we were going to be together. We all can't wake up looking casket ready. I was a real bitch.

I fixed Kente an egg white omelet with mushrooms, peppers and mozzarella, turkey sausage, a fruit bowl, whole wheat toast and a glass of mango juice. I knew that he was more health-conscious than I was, so I fixed a breakfast more suited to him. Because if it was just for me, it would be full of everything fattening. I plated his food and set everything on a tray and carefully walked towards my room.

Kente was sprawled across the bed with the blankets covering him from the waist down. I licked my lips as I eyed the smoothness of his chocolate skin that was exposed. He was still naked underneath the sheets and I was hoping that he would stay that way because I wanted another sample of what he had to offer before the kids came back from Jason's.

"Damn, you cooked for me? Shit, I must've laid the pipe if you making me breakfast and not trying to get beautified and shit," Kente said, stretching. He woke up as soon as he smelled the food when I walked in the room.

"I'm only going to say this once. You need to see the real me at all times. I don't always look like I'm ready for the stage. I'm human and I have a lot of fucking hair, so this is what I look like most mornings. I'm not ever going to front like my lashes and makeup are flawless at all times. I wake up just like this. Either take it or leave it," I stated.

"Well, I'll take breakfast. Then I want to take you and see if you can hang from your shower rod," he said with a devilish smirk. I grinned because he knew just how to get my day started right.

Jason

S hit was getting deep. I was falling deeper and deeper in love with Felicity, but I still hadn't told her about my other business. My mom kept warning me that shit was going to blow up in my face and shit almost happened when I got a strange phone call in the middle of the night from one of my workers while Felicity was over.

Someone on the bottle team was stealing pills. It was just my luck that one of these niggas would start getting high. I told each one of these niggas that they had to remain clean and sober on shift, no matter what. I didn't play that, oh, it's just a little weed here and there. You were not allowed to smoke or drink while on shift. I didn't give a fuck what you did in your spare time, but my time was only about the money.

"What was that about?" Felicity asked me when I ended the call.

"Nothing. Just something was wrong with the inventory count. I have to go in there first thing in the morning and get shit straight. I don't want to go down there this time of night. If I do, shit will get ugly," I honestly admitted.

"Well, alrighty then. Maybe I should go home, then. You probably have to get up extra early to handle business," she said with an attitude.

"I'm sorry sweetheart. Don't leave. It's just that I have a lot going on and shit down at the club is a stress that I just don't need," I admitted.

"What the hell is wrong, then? You can talk to me about anything," she told me.

"I got this in the mail," I said, deflecting from the real reason why I was stressed.

I got up from my bed and walked over to my desk. I grabbed the heavy envelope and walked back over to Felicity. I handed it to her and sat next to where she was laying on the bed. When she opened the envelope and saw the invitation from Raven, I swear that her face contorted into another person. She threw the invitation on the bed and what she said next made the hair on my arms stand up.

"If I go to this freak show, I am not responsible for my actions," she said.

"I already know. I just wanted you to see the bullshit. I want to go just to show her that we're not fazed by her. I want her to know that she's not even a thought in our heads. I've been over her ass, so I want to go," I said.

I meant every word. Plus, I had to have a word with Ramon. I wondered if he knew what a snake Javad was and that he was using him and his connections to protect himself. Shit was about to go left in Javad's life and Ramon's family offered him the protection that he desperately needs.

"Hey, come back from wherever you just went," Felicity said, snapping me from my thoughts.

"My bad. I was thinking about business again. This thing at the club has my mind all over the place," I lied.

"Look, why don't you go and handle your business. I'll stay here while you get things straight. I don't need you distracted," she told me.

"Thanks, babe. You really are my rider," I told her. I kissed her on the head before grabbing my stuff and heading out.

I shot my mom a text and let her know what was going on, and she told me that she was on the way to the club already. That's when I knew that shit was worse than I was told. My mom never came out unless shit was getting thick. I guess this was one of the few times the queen had to step off her throne.

I pulled up to the club in no time it seemed like. The main parking lot across from the club was deserted during what my mom called booty call hours. She always said that there was nothing open this time of night but legs and 7-Eleven. I laughed to myself at that thought as I pulled around the back of the club where the employees parked. I saw the cars of my entire team, including the lieutenants.

I breathed heavily because I knew that the Grim Reaper was standing in the shadows somewhere in the building. There was going to be at least one dead body before the night was over with. I just wanted this to be done before the sun came up. I knew that if I didn't make it back before sunrise, Felicity was going to have questions. Then I would have to tell her about my double life.

"I don't know how this shit managed to go on for so long. Now I had to get out of my bed and come all the way out here," I heard my mom say.

"Well, we didn't want to worry you or the boss man. We thought we could get it under control, but it's just getting out of hand," I heard one of my men say before I stepped into view from the shadows.

"Well, the moment you noticed the shortage, you should have told me. The fact that we've lost almost ten thousand dollars in product is unacceptable. So, what do you think should happen?" I asked, knowing full-blown well that someone was about to die this night.

"I'll take the punishment. This was my team, and I fucked up. Just make sure that my girl and kids are straight. Make sure they can have an open casket," the same man said before kneeling down with his back to me.

This was the type of G-shit that I respected. This man knew that he fucked up and was willing to give up his life for this shit. Most niggas now would try and throw everyone else in their crew under the bus, but Mike was a true soldier. And for that, I couldn't end his life. He proved himself with his willingness to lay his life down for his fuck up.

"Get up, Mike. You're not dying today. But this nigga right here is," I said before putting a bullet right through Mike's right-hand man's head.

The way this bitch nigga was sweating and twitching, I knew that he was the one using the product and stealing money. He was willing to let his boy die for his fuck ups and that shit was flawed. Everyone stood there and looked at me waiting for an explanation. While I had men clean up the body and send it to be found somewhere, I sat down and started talking.

"This was a clear reminder that I will always find shit out. That nigga was disloyal. Not only to me, but to the man that trusted him with his life. He was willing to let Mike sit there and die to cover his own ass. Mike, you just proved yourself to be the most loyal nigga I know. For that, you will be rewarded. You will be taking over here with the shipments and your trap is shut down for now. We start re-training these niggas tomorrow. Be grateful that all of you didn't end up in body bags tonight," I said, ending the meeting.

"I need a word with you, son," my mom said, and had me follow her to my office. "You need to tell Felicity about this. Too much is going on, and eventually she will catch on. The fact that I had to come out here, should be a big indicator that this shit will blow up in your face! That girl deserves better than this. You know I can't stand Raven, but you kept the same secret from her. You can't possibly think that you can have a successful relationship with this big of a secret," my mom said as soon as I closed the door to my office.

"I know. I'm telling her as soon as I get home. I snapped on her tonight and she didn't deserve that. I hope she sticks around and rides with me after this," I admitted.

"Just go home and talk to that girl. Because you don't want me to do it, and you know I will," my mom said.

I kissed her on the cheek and told her that I would call her later. She told me to get home safely and that she would stay at my condo in the city since it was so late, and she lived so far out. I told her to make herself at home and that she didn't need to come into the office. She needed a day off for once and I needed to be in the office handling business more.

When I finally made it back to my house, the sun was starting to rise in the sky. I knew that Felicity would be beyond pissed and I had a lot of explaining to do. It was time for me to be completely open and honest with her, something that I had been wanting to do for months.

"What the hell! You could at least call and let me know you're alive! I have to do promo shoots for the show today and I've been up all night worried about your ass!" Felicity screamed as soon as I walked through the front door.

"Baby, I know and I'm sorry. Some real shit went down and I had to do something that I didn't want to do," I said as I spoke in circles.

"What do you mean by that? You're starting to scare me," she said with her voice starting to shake.

"I'm getting to that. Look, I haven't been completely honest with you about how I get all of my money. I wanted to keep you away from this part of my life, but how can I be with you and not let you all the way in?" I started, and then explained to her about my pill operation.

She just sat there at my kitchen table stone-faced while I talked. She didn't respond when I finished. She just got up and fixed coffee and put a plate of croissants on the table. I was nervously sitting and waiting for her to respond. She poured two cups of coffee and then finally sat back down.

"So, when are you going to shut it down or pass it on? You're so successful legally, you don't need this street shit anymore. I can't see myself living the life of some hood queen like in the books that I read. I don't want to worry that one day the feds are going to come busting in and taking everything from you and your mom," she said, throwing me.

"I never really thought about it. I mean, I tried to go legit, but the pills and shit got me so much money that I just kept at it. It was just second nature to me. I guess I need to really think about passing the torch," I replied back after a moment.

"You do. Especially if you want me and Avalon in your life. I gotta go," she said. She finished her coffee and rinsed her cup out before putting it in the dishwasher.

She gave me a quick peck on the lips, and I watched her hips sway as she walked out the door. I knew that I needed to make some changes and fast if I wanted to keep Felicity in my life. It was time to man the fuck up.

Felicity

The hits just kept coming at my ass. First this dumb ass hoe Raven sends a wedding invitation and now Jason's secret business. I knew that he was a street nigga when I met him, but I thought that he had left that part of his life behind him. Silly of me to think that there was a man out there that would be as honest and open with me as I was with him.

This was why I had remained celibate for all this time. I was perfectly fine being in my little bubble with Avalon and Mama Gina. I knew that Jason loved me and was a good man, but I wasn't cut out for the street shit. I saw what drugs and alcohol did to my parents and I vowed that I would stay as far away from that lifestyle as I could. So, Jason needed to decide what was more important. The streets or me and his real business.

"Fefe! Can I talk to you for a minute?" I heard Dylan's voice before I saw him.

He was standing in the parking lot looking like a lost puppy. I sighed deeply because the last thing I wanted to do was talk to this man. He caused my life so much havoc and pain from one ten-minute incident in the backseat of his car. I walked to where he was standing and stood a safe distance away from him as I waited for him to talk.

"You have exactly ninety seconds to speak your piece," I said.

"Look, I haven't been the best guy over the years. I let you walk away and raise our daughter on your own. I just wanted to come to you as a man and apologize to you. That, and to let you know that I am checking myself into rehab, so I won't be able to see our daughter for a while. I don't want her to see me detoxing," he said to me.

My face and stance softened towards him. He looked and sounded sincere, so I decided to hear him out some more. He told me about his visit with his parents and how his father was getting remarried to his former manager. I would say that I was surprised, but it was a long-standing rumor that his father and his manager were sleeping with each other for years.

"Well, I don't know what else to say, but good luck, and I wish you nothing but the best," I said and started to walk away.

"I love you and I always will," he yelled out as I walked into the building. I didn't stop moving until I got on the elevator heading up to The Closet. I knew that if I had stopped and responded to Dylan, nothing but trouble would come of it.

I put him in the back of my mind and let Rhea help style me for the promo shoot for the show. I was still frazzled from Dylan's confession, so I wasn't paying attention to what Rhea was saying to me. She had been pulling outfits out and showing them to me for at least five minutes before she said something to me.

"You must have some heavy shit on your mind if you were about to let me put your ass in plaid," she said, finally getting my attention.

"And I would bury your ass alive," I said.

"What's going on with you? I have never seen you this distracted before," she asked me.

"I'm just tired. I didn't get any sleep last night. I was up reading this book called *Bad Boys Do It Better* and I couldn't put it down," I said, giving her only half the truth.

"Oh! I read that one months ago! You need to read the whole series and the spin-off. All I know is, I need a nigga like Luke," Rhea said, and we talked about the book while we found my looks for the day.

When I was satisfied with my fashion choices, I went to hair and makeup to get beautified. I saw the one co-star that I couldn't stand sitting in the chair next to where I was planning on sitting. I couldn't stand this woman for the very reason that she constantly tried to fuck my man every time I turned my head. I knew that if I said something that she wouldn't be asked to return for the next season. But that was a diva antic that I refused to be reduced to. She couldn't act well anyway, and her screen time had been reduced the more we shot.

"Trouble in paradise? I mean, those suitcases under your eyes are very telling," she taunted.

"Bitch, please. All that means is that the dick you try to get with no win, keeps my ass screaming all night. Edgeless wombat," I muttered.

"That wasn't a palm leaf, that was the whole damn tree of shade," Don, my makeup artist, said with a snicker.

"She's telling the truth, though. I've heard them," Ginger said as she walked into the makeup room.

"Oh, and bitch, if you ever send a picture of your mangled pussy to my man again, your edges won't be the only thing missing," Ginger said. She walked over to the woman and snatched her head back by her dry ass weave.

"Ouch! You're hurting me! You crazy bitch!" Katy screamed. Ginger still had a mean grip on her hair, and every time that Katy yelled, Ginger pulled tighter.

"Chile, let her go. You know she can't bust a grape in a blender. She's just a hoe that's about to get written out anyway, with her non-acting ass," I said, trying to calm the situation down.

"At least I didn't fuck the boss to get the part," Katy spat. This bitch was still talking shit even though she was about to get her neck snapped.

"What the fuck is going on in here!" Jason roared. He walked in the room while we were all trying to pry Ginger's vice grip from Katy's hair.

"Somebody needs to check this hoe, and I am somebody," Ginger said. When she said that, my ass fell out laughing.

I knew I was supposed to be stopping my girl from catching a case, but the shit she just said was too fucking funny. Jason glared at me for a second, but then focused on detangling Ginger's fingers from Katy's head. He managed to separate the two women, but not before Ginger sent her open hand across Katy's face.

"This is not the WWE. I don't care who started it, this shit can't happen here," Jason yelled.

"But she attacked me!" Katy whined.

"Do I look like I give a fuck? All your ass does is try and fuck every man you come across and disrupt the set. I swear if it wasn't for the fact that I owed your brother a favor, your ass wouldn't have made it past episode two. Just know that this season will be your only season," he told Katy.

"Like I give a fuck. You act like you're Tyler Perry or some shit. I don't even want to be a part of this low budget shit any fucking way!" Katy boldly yelled back.

I saw Jason's jaw flex and I knew that shit was about to get ugly, so I stepped in to defuse the situation. This wasn't what he wanted for himself. He didn't need any heat coming his way. Especially while he was still in the game like he was. I guess it was time for me to step up and show my man that I still had his back.

"Well, then you must know that your services are no longer needed here at Relevant. Once we shoot your final episodes, you don't have to worry about showing up to set. Please leave your passes with personnel by the end of the day. And don't make me step out of my character. I actually was in the Army and I don't mind using my training on your ass," I said calmly.

Katy looked like she wanted to say something, but I think that she saw the look on Jason's face and thought better of it. She stalked out of the makeup room and went down the hall back to hair to get her weave fixed. After that, things settled down and I sat back in my seat to get my face beat to the gods. I explained to Jason what went down before he walked in and he just shook his head at us.

"As much as that bitch deserved it, y'all got to move smarter. You can't beat up bitches for sending pussy pics and shit. Look at Cardi B and the fact that she in all that shit for tearing up a strip club. All that beef shit can end your career before it begins," he advised.

"I know, and that's why I tried to keep it professional. But that hoe just don't know when to shut the fuck up. She won't last long after this shit, that's for sure," I agreed.

Ginger and I agreed that we would both try and keep our tempers in check. Well, at least until I finished up the photoshoot this afternoon. After the way I checked that bitch, I was sure that she would be making slick ass comments the whole shoot, but I would rise above and get through the day.

The shoot went better than I thought. Katy was quiet the whole time and just did as the photographer said. I guess once she was done with legal, she knew that she didn't have a case since she was known for trying to get with many of the men on the set of the show. She would be the one facing a sexual harassment suit if she tried to sue the studio.

I rushed to change and get to Jason as soon as the photographer said that we were done. I slipped out of the Chanel jumpsuit and back into my Fashion Nova jeans and Champion crop top. I slid my feet into my white Air Forces and then hopped on the elevator towards Jason's office. I wanted to talk to my man more about his situation and tell him about Dylan before someone else did.

"Do you have an appointment with Mr. Miller?" a young woman around my age asked from Brady's desk. He must've been out sick because Jason knew that he wasn't allowed another female assistant, and Brady was actually the best assistant in the game.

"Bitch, please. I don't need an appointment," I stated and started to walk towards Jason's office.

"You do if I say so," she said and poked out her silicone filled double D-cup breasts. Her skirt was damn near exposing her pussy and I knew her ass didn't have on any panties because I could smell her foul odor coming from between her legs.

"You must not want a job because last time I checked, I was the boss' woman. Now move, hoe, before I move you." I pushed right past her and stormed into Jason's office.

"Get rid of that hoe and tell Brady to get his ass back here yesterday," I fumed.

"I didn't send for her, she was here this morning when I got here. Brady had a family emergency and won't be back for a week. I'll get another temp because that chick messed up most of my messages and almost made me miss a meeting with the Jack Daniel's rep," he said. I let out a sigh of relief and then went and sat on his lap.

"Dylan was here this morning. He told me that he was going to rehab. I told him good luck. But when I was walking away, he said that he loved me. I didn't say anything, I just kept on walking," I told him.

"That muhfucka really getting on my nerves," he said.

"I know. But I had to tell you. If there was one thing that I learned from the last time he pulled a stunt, it was to let you know before someone else did. I want complete honesty between us from here on out. No more secrets," I told him, looking him square in the eyes.

"No more secrets," he promised me. I just hoped that he kept his word.

Ginger

My hand was still hurting while I drove back home to meet the girls' buses. I was still fuming over the photo that I found in Kente's phone. I knew that he hadn't opened the DM, but the fact that this hoe felt comfortable enough to send it sent me in a rage. I knew that I was going to have to talk to Kente about it eventually because it was all caught on camera for the show. This was just the drama the producers were looking for and it wasn't fake like some of the other drama on the show.

I pulled into my driveway and saw Kente's Ferrari parked by the curb. He was standing by my front door with a sheepish look on his face. I smiled and took my time getting out of the car. I was trying to tell my good girl to calm her ass down and stop dancing. Just the sight of that man made me cream in my panties.

"You might as well bring your sexy ass on over here and stop hiding," he called out loud enough for my neighbors to hear.

"Will you hush? My neighbors can hear you," I whispered loudly when I got close enough to him.

"Like I give a fuck. If they knew what was good for them, they'd close their blinds while I do this," he said before sucking the air out of my mouth.

He kissed me so deeply and passionately that I felt my legs give out from under me. Every time that man touched me, my body went into sensory overload. He made me feel like a woman in every form. He gave me confidence that I lost the moment Devante left my ass for another woman. I was becoming well known as Kente's girl while still maintaining my privacy for the most part.

"I want you so bad, Gin. I promise you that I have never even said hi to that bitch. I only want you," he said to me, and I believed him.

I was about to kiss him again, but the sound of the bus stopping at the corner prevented the second act of our little show. I heard Clark, Juliette and Avalon's mouths before I saw them. The three of them came charging down towards my house laughing and talking loud as hell. We couldn't understand what they were saying, but whatever it was, it had to be something good for them to be so loud.

"Auntie Ginger, guess what?" Avalon asked when they made it to where Kente and I were standing.

"What, angel?" I asked.

"We're going to Six Flags! I've never been before! Can you and Mommy chaperone?" she asked.

"I will, but you have to ask your mom when she gets home later. And I haven't been there, either," I admitted.

I ushered the girls in the house so they could get started on their homework and Kente and I could talk. I wanted to get started on dinner and try to come to some sort of understanding about my relationship with Kente. I had to know that he was serious about being with me and only me. I didn't share my food, much less my man, so he needed to be sure that he would be loyal to me and my daughters.

"I can tell you wanted to talk to me alone," Kente said as soon as we were alone in the kitchen.

"And you would be right," I responded as I pulled out flour tortillas, a bowl of pork that I was marinating, vegetables and spices. I was going to make my version of tacos el pastor.

"I know you think that I'm like all of the other entertainers out there. You know, sleeping with any and everybody, but I'm not like that at all. When I'm with a woman, I'm with that woman. Yes, I've fucked bitches while I was single. But you can ask my ex, I never cheated on her. She just couldn't handle my schedule and we decided to end things. That was two years ago and we're still cool. In fact, she's about to get married to some regular type guy, and I'm happy for her," he explained.

"You got me there. Because she has never once mentioned anything bad about you to the blogs. She does seem like a nice woman and everything, so I can only trust your word. But let me tell you this. If you even feel like you might cheat, call me and break up with me. Don't do anything that will have me out here looking stupid," I warned.

"Deal. Now can I seal our deal with a kiss?" he asked before crossing the room and covering my lips with his.

Dylan

TELLING FELICITY that I was going to rehab was the hardest thing that I had ever done. But I had to do it if I was going to have a shot at winning her back. I needed to be sober so that I could focus on what I needed to do to get Jason out of her life for good.

"Okay, Mr. James. Do you have anything on you today? Any pills, weed, alcohol or other substances?" the woman doing my intake asked me while she searched through my bags.

"A bottle of Vicodin," I told her. She nodded and then pulled out two more pill bottles and a bag of coke.

She shook her head like she knew that I was lying. I was sure that she had probably seen and heard it all before and knew all of the tricks to the trade. She took all of my drugs and walked into another room where she handed them over to someone else. She made me strip down to my boxers and follow her into the bathroom where she handed me a cup to piss in.

"Why do I have to be in my draws, though?" I asked her.

"It's policy. We take extra precaution here to make sure you don't try and fake your test. We've seen it all," she explained while I emptied my bladder.

After pissing in the cup, she took the cup with her gloved hand and dipped a bunch of test strips in it to see what was in my system. My cheeks flushed red when I saw that I came back positive for every type of drug. She gave me a reassuring look that let me know that she wasn't judging me at all. After all, this was a rehab center.

"Okay, now that we know what's in your system, we know how to treat your detox process," the woman, whose name tag read Star, told me.

She had me follow her as she showed me the grounds. The place was beautiful. It sat on a secluded part of Key West and we had the perfect view of the ocean. It was built like a five-star resort with swimming pools, a gym, a library and at least four kitchens that they kept fully stocked. We walked into my suite and I was amazed.

It was set up like a studio apartment. There was a full-sized bed, a sofa, television, kitchen table for two, a small kitchenette and a full bathroom. The walls were blank, but I was told that I could decorate the room any way that I wanted during my stay. She let me know that she was going to leave me to unpack and that the first group session was in two hours, before closing the door and leaving me to my thoughts.

"I guess I better get started," I said to myself and put my clothes away.

. . .

"Good evening, everyone. My name is Dave, and I'm an addict," a man said.

We were sitting in the common area in a circle and he was standing in the center. It was the first meeting for all of the new residents to get us used to being in rehab. Some were repeaters, but for most of us, this was our first time. I just wanted this to be a one and done with me. Dave asked each one of us to give our story and I was nervous because most of mine was already out there for the world to see.

"My name is Dylan. I'm here because I want my family back," was all I said before sitting down.

Everyone looked at me like they wanted me to say more, but that was all they were going to get from me. I just wanted to do my ninety days, get my chip and then get my family and career back. I was only doing this so that I would look good in Felicity's eyes. No one could tell me anything different.

"You know, it can make things easier if you just open up and trust the process," a pretty woman said to me after group was over.

I was stuck on my words for a moment as I took her in. She stood about five-foot six and had deep chocolate skin. She had dark brown eyes and her black hair was cut low with silky curls. Her diamond-shaped face held a small button nose, full bow-shaped lips and large almond-shaped eyes. My eyes trailed down and caught an eyeful of her thick hips, tiny waist, perky breasts and round ass.

"Hello! You can eye-fuck me later, Dylan James, aka Adam Newman," she said.

"My bad. I didn't get your name. And I thought that no one would remember me from that," I said.

"My name is Christina. And *The Young and the Restless* was my mom's favorite show. I used to watch it with my mom every day. Well, until I decided that sucking on a glass dick was better than my mom's hugs," she said wistfully.

We started walking towards the main kitchen so that we could get something to eat. I realized that I hadn't eaten all day and that I was starving. I opened the fridge and saw the ingredients to make one hell of a hoagie. I put everything on the counter and grabbed a plate and utensils while Christina sat and watched with an amused look on her face.

"You might want to eat something lighter. Withdrawal is a bitch and let me tell you, you are not going to like tasting that again," she suggested.

"How many times have you done this?" I asked, being nosy. She didn't look like she needed to be here, but neither did I, I thought.

"This is my third time in ten years. I'm only twenty-eight, but I started using at fourteen. It started with weed, then molly, then coke, then crack. The only thing that I didn't do was heroin of any form. I'm here this time because my depression was starting to get the best of me, and I felt like I might start using again," she explained to me.

"I honestly would have pegged you as one of the counselors here. You look so put together," I said, giving her a compliment.

"You do realize that most of the counselors and staff here are recovering addicts. They've been clean at least ten years. That's why this place is so successful. It's also the reason why I chose to come here," she told me.

"That's why they seemed to know all of my moves. I tried to sneak some shit in and got caught," I admitted.

"You met Star. She's the mom of the place. Matter of fact, she's the owner. She said she opened this place after her son died from an overdose. She said that she wished that there was a place like this for her son years ago. She felt that if there was, he would still be alive. But maybe his death was her reason for living and saving the rest of us," she said.

Christina was deep as shit. She held my attention the entire time while I ate my food. I liked talking to her and I felt more relaxed being around her. She was making me feel like I might actually get something out of this rehab shit. Not to mention she was bad as fuck.

Before I knew it, two hours had passed, and we were still sitting in the dining hall talking. We had cleaned up our dishes and were walking to our rooms. I saw that we were on the same floor. I grew excited at the prospect of seeing her every morning and talking to her more. There was something different about her that I liked, and I wanted to know more.

"I'll see you for breakfast in the morning, if you're up to it. If not, I'll come and check on you," Christina said before giving me a side hug and walking off.

I watched her walk away and felt my dick grow hard as her ass jiggled in the sweats she was wearing. I was imagining how good my dick would feel in her pussy while I hit it from behind. I rushed in my room so no one would see me lusting after another resident since intimate relationships were strictly prohibited during our stay.

I also realized that I hadn't thought about Felicity once since I started a conversation with Christina. That wasn't good at all. I didn't need anything distracting me from my end goal. I definitely had to keep my distance from Christina.

Raven

All my plans and hard work were finally coming together. Jason confirmed that he and Felicity were coming to my wedding, and I was over the moon excited. Jason's little bitch would be sniffing dirt before I made the first cut on my wedding cake. And I had Ramon to thank for that.

"My love, you look amazing," Ramon complimented me as I walked down the stairs.

I was wearing a white vintage Versace dress with matching gold heels. I had my hair freshly dyed a soft, light brown, and it was pulled up into an elegant bun on the top of my head. I blushed a bit because this man found a way to compliment me every day and I was starting to fall for this man despite me fighting it.

"You don't look so bad yourself," I said back.

Ramon was wearing a charcoal gray Armani suit and black loafers on his feet. His hair was freshly lined up and he had grown his hair out long enough for it to fit into a man bun. I saw his diamond-filled Rolex blinding me as I made my way to him. I stretched out my arms and he took my hands in his as he looked me up and down.

"I don't know if it's right to let you out of the house looking this good," he said.

We were going to some huge event in downtown Atlanta and I was finally going to be able to show myself to the world for the first time in nearly a year. I mean, I was posting on social media constantly, and I had regained my sponsorships with some of my old brands. The world knew that I was back and better than ever, but no one had seen me in public for months and it was time for me to make an appearance.

"It's time for people to know that nothing will ever keep me down. Plus, I make you look good," I joked flirtatiously.

"That you do. Well then, it's time to show off my future wife." He hooked my arm in his and we walked out the door to a stretch limo waiting outside for us.

We pulled up to the convention center downtown, and I noticed that this was a red-carpet affair. This was why Ramon was so bent on me looking my best. Not only was my dress amazing, I was dripping in nearly ten million dollars' worth of diamonds on my neck, ears and wrists. We looked like Atlanta royalty when we stepped out of the limo and into the flashes of the cameras.

We were bombarded with questions about who the man on my arm was and where I had been. I just smiled coyly and posed in my dress. I made sure to name every designer that I had on before I said anything to the reporters.

"Well, this is Ramon Negron, and he is the man that has changed my life for the better. I am so proud to say that in the very near future he will be my husband," I proudly stated to the press.

"So, you're not fazed by the relationship that your ex-husband has with your old boy toy's baby momma?" I heard someone ask.

"Why should I be? I mean, look at me and look at my man. Why should I be worried about someone that is clearly my past?" I responded, even though I wanted to knock her teeth down her throat.

"Good move, baby. Never let them see you sweat. Now let's go and have a good time," Ramon whispered in my ear. The feel of his breath on my ear and the smell of his Clive Christian No. 1 cologne had my pussy tingling.

We walked into the building and I was in awe at how many people were there. It was a charity ball for AIDS research and that was something that was actually near and dear to my heart since my brother was diagnosed with HIV when he was twenty-one. My brother was the only person in the world that I really gave a fuck about. That was until Ramon came into my life.

"Raven Natal! I thought that was you," I heard a familiar voice say.

I turned to face a person that I wished to have never seen again. Naima was standing in front of me with this shit-eating smirk on her face. She was still beautiful, but I'm sure she got some perverse pleasure out of seeing me squirm a bit in my heels.

"Naima. You look well," I said to her, returning her grin.

"I come in peace. I'm just here to tell you that you look amazing and that I was always hoping to see you on top. Congratulations on your engagement. You are glowing. Are you sure that you aren't expecting?" she asked me.

"I seriously doubt that. But thank you. And I am really sorry for what I did to you all those years ago. I wasn't in a clear head," I apologized sincerely for the first time in my life.

After that we caught up on how life was for us and I found myself actually enjoying her company. We were pretty much left to ourselves because our dates had left us alone to mingle and make business connections. I watched Ramon work his magic and decided that I could do the same thing and try to revive my career. Maybe being Ramon's wife wouldn't be such a bad thing after all.

Felicity

F ilming for the show wrapped up finally and I was so happy. Now that I finally had a break, I was ready to get into the studio and work on my album fully. It had been a long few months and I was welcoming not having to get up at the ass crack of dawn to cake my face with makeup and wear clothes that I would never wear in real life. Plus, I got to hang out with my favorite person in the world, Avalon.

"I see someone is taking advantage of her time off," Mama Gina said to me when I finally woke up and came in the kitchen.

"You have no idea, Ma," I said as I poured myself a cup of coffee.

"I'm not knocking it at all. Shit, you were working six days a week for damn near six months. We barely saw you. I mean, we understood that you were working, but we missed you," she said.

My eyes misted over, and I damn near ran to give her a hug. This woman was such a godsend in my life. She brought me up and help raise me to be a woman while I was trying to be a mom and a teenager at the same time. She made me believe in myself and let me know that I was doing everything right. Where my own parents failed me, she was the one that was a real parent to me. I owed this woman my life and I was going to spend as much time as possible making sure that she knew it.

"Ma, I swear that I'm going to make time. With shooting over for right now, all I have to do is spend a couple of hours a day in the studio. I can do that while Avalon is in school and then be home to fix dinner. That way you and Kenny can have time to be alone with each other," I explained.

"Now you don't have to do all of that. Kenny and I are doing just fine. He loves Avalon and treats her like she's one of his own grandchildren," she told me.

I really liked Kenny for her. He was a patient man and his kids loved Mama Gina. I was hoping that he would propose soon. They seemed to be just as in love as Jason and I were, if not more. Kenny was always sending flowers and little gifts for Mama Gina. And when he wasn't doing that, he was here helping her with Avalon while I was on the set.

"Ma, I know you say that you two are just fine, but I want you to be more than fine. I want you and Kenny to walk down the aisle," I admitted.

"Chile, bye! I'm hoping that Jason will wise up and put a ring on that finger. He needs to put a down payment on that cow and stop renting the milk machine," she said, making me choke on my coffee.

"That's it. I'm getting dressed and going over to Ginger's. We're supposed to meet up with Megan for lunch," I explained. Mama Gina nodded her head and went back to her breakfast.

I quickly took a shower and put on a pair of jeans and a white sweater. I slid my feet into a pair of wheat Timberlands and grabbed a short, tan leather jacket and matching purse before heading out. I decided to not wear makeup and give my face a break for a while. I grabbed the keys for my Tesla that Jason had gifted me and headed for my car. I decided to give my Audi to Mama Gina so that she would have something nice to drive around in.

Ginger met me by my car, and I had to give it to her. She was working the hell out of the denim jumpsuit and red pumps. She had her hair pulled back in a tight ponytail and she was wearing matching red shades and a red leather jacket. Her ass was on full display and I knew that she was going to have heads turning. I was shocked that she could fit that outfit over her ass, that thing was that big.

"Damn, girl! You're about to be killing them out there. I guess Kente been hitting that ass right," I joked as we got in the car.

"Girl!" was all she could say before fanning herself. She was all smiles and I knew she had finally broken her celibacy and gave up the pussy.

"Is the dick that good?" I had to ask. Shit, I had been giving her all the tea about how Jason had my ass spread eagle, so she was about to spill hers.

"Girl, that nigga is working with a monster! And then he has the nerve to have a curve in his dick. That nigga had my uterus pushed up in my throat," she exclaimed.

I damn near swerved off the road with her revelation. My girl was back in the saddle again, literally. I was happy for her and I knew that Kente was the one for her. From the moment that he saw her during our first studio session, he was a man on a mission. He told me in that session that Ginger was going to be his wife one day, and I believed him. I told him that I was going to help him get her, and now look at us. Happy and in love with two amazing men.

We pulled up to the OLG restaurant where we were meeting Megan. She had been cooped up in the house for weeks since Kwame injured his Achille's tendon during a game against the Oklahoma City Thunder. Kwame forced her out of the house so that she could get a breather while his mother looked after him and baby Kenyon.

The paparazzi was out in full effect and I knew that questions would be coming fast and furious. I parked my car as quickly as possible, and Ginger and I rushed past all of the cameras into the restaurant. We saw

Megan sitting in a booth in the back waiting for us with a bottle of white wine chilling in a bucket.

"I feel so underdressed sitting with you two hoes," I commented as I sat down.

Megan was wearing DVF from head to toe. Her hair was braided underneath a honey blonde lace bob that curled around her face and brought out the gold in her eyes. She didn't look like she had just had a baby a year ago. She snapped right back, and I was a little jealous. It took me two years to get my body right after I had Avalon.

"And yet, you're the finest one in the room. Now hush and order some chicken so that I can eat your greens," Megan said as we caught up.

She was telling me about Kenyon and how he was toddling around all over the house and getting into everything. She looked tired despite the way she had flawlessly applied her makeup. I knew that she was stressed out being Kwame's main caregiver, especially with this being his contract year.

"I have some more news for you guys. I'm pregnant again," Megan announced.

"Hush your mouth and slap me blue," Ginger said.

"I knew that would happen sooner or later. The way you snapped back after you had Kenyon, I'm shocked that it hasn't happened sooner," I said.

"I know the fuck she didn't," Ginger snapped. We looked over to where she was looking, and there she was in the flesh: Raven.

I had to admit, she looked amazing. Her hair was thick and healthy looking, and she had a glow about her. She looked softer than the woman that I had the displeasure of meeting a year ago. She was sitting with a woman that I recognized from *America's Next Top Model*, but that wasn't my reason for looking.

I wanted to make sure that Raven knew that I saw her and that she didn't faze my ass one bit. I wanted her to see me looking good and feeling good. I wanted her to know that no matter what game she thought she was playing, that I was always going to be two steps ahead of her. She was playing checkers, while I was playing chess. I knew all about her plan to try and kidnap and murder me on her wedding night. Little did she know that may possibly be her last night on earth if she didn't call the shit off.

"You want to leave, boo? Just say the word and we can go to STK," Ginger said.

"Please. That bitch don't move me. There isn't one soul out here that would make me turn down this sweet potato pie," I said as I dug into my dessert.

After we finished lunch, we decided to go shopping since we were having so much fun together. I wanted to get Jason something nice for being so patient with me all of this time. He had done so much for me, that I felt he deserved something more than just what was between my legs.

We stopped by Cartier and I decided to buy him a necklace, a cocktail shaker and this pocket watch that I saw him admiring the other week. We also went into Louis Vuitton and I bought him a new carry-on bag and laptop case. I knew that I spent a grip on him, but he was worth it.

"Okay, ladies, I have to get back home to my men and give my mother-in-law a break," Megan said, hugging us goodbye.

"We need to have a girls' night soon. Megan will be showing soon and then it will be just the two of us, unless Jason knocks you up, too," Ginger said as I navigated my car back to Lawrenceville.

"Bitch, bye! Avalon is all I need. I don't need another child right now," I said.

"Well, you should think about it. Avalon will be nine soon and I know she gets bored when the girls aren't around. She needs a sibling before she gets too old to want to be around a baby," Ginger advised.

I didn't say anything else. I just let the music play while I thought about what Ginger said. I wasn't opposed to having another baby. I just wanted things to be right in my life before I even thought about taking that next step. Like not having Raven and her revenge plot in the back of my mind stressing me out.

Raven

I magine my surprise to see Felicity out with her minions while I was having lunch with Naima. I just sat back and enjoyed watching Felicity squirm a bit. I knew she saw me, and I didn't care. I was living my best life and I had a man that wanted to give me the world.

Ramon and I were doing great since the gala a few weeks ago. I was now in full wedding planning mode and it was fun. I was having the time of my life because Ramon told me that there was no budget and that I could spend what I wanted to make our day amazing.

"How many dresses would you like me to pull for you to try on, and what's your budget?" the salesgirl asked me.

"There is no budget. And I want any dress that's full of bling and sexy as hell. I'm thinking I might get four dresses. I want to have different looks for different parts of the day," I stated.

I was waiting on Naima to show up and help me pick out a dress. Other than my maid Nessa, Naima was the only female that I had around that I could consider a friend. I felt a twinge of remorse because I hadn't reached out to Charisse at all, and we had been through it all together. Instinctively, I pulled out my phone and dialed Charisse's number, hoping that it was the same and that she would pick up.

"Hello?" I heard her light voice say once she answered. I took a deep breath and finally spoke.

"Hi, Charisse. How are you?" I managed to say.

"Raven? Oh my goodness! I saw you in the blogs and it was like seeing a ghost. You look amazing," she gushed, reminding me how much I missed her.

Charisse was more than my manager, she was my best friend. She was the one that was able to talk me down from so much shit. She kept me in line when I was going so far to the left that I was back at my right. She was my sounding board and I was hers. I knew all of her darkest secrets and vice versa.

"Thank you. Look, I know I have been a horrible person these last few years, so I want to apologize. And I also want to know if you're busy because I'm at the dress shop looking for wedding gowns, and I need another opinion," I admitted.

"Text me the address and I'll be there as soon as I can," she said, and we disconnected our call.

Twenty minutes later, Charisse and Naima were sitting around, drinking champagne while I slipped into the first dress. It was a mermaid style dress covered in Swarovski crystals. The bodice was cut low and exposed my breasts tastefully. It hugged my waist tight and fit over my hips before flaring out into a six-foot train. It was snow white and gorgeous.

The salesgirl put a crystal tiara and a sheer veil with the same crystals along the border on my head. When I looked at myself in the mirror, I wanted to break down in tears. I had never in my life seen myself look as beautiful as I did in that moment. I realized while I was in that dress that I was in love with Ramon. That was why I looked and felt the way I did.

I wasn't even sure if going through with the plan to kidnap and murder Felicity was worth it anymore. She clearly made Jason happy. I was just with him for his money and status. But now I had a man that had ten times of what Jason had. I never had to work another day in my life if I didn't want to and I was cool with that. I was thinking that I might just let them be at this point.

"Oh, you're so gorgeous!" both Charisse and Naima exclaimed when I walked out of the dressing room.

I twirled around the large pedestal, so they were able to get the full effect of the dress. By the looks on their faces, I knew that I had found the dress that I would walk down the aisle in. Now it was time to find a dress for pictures, the cake cutting, and then one to dance the night away in.

"Okay, ladies. Next week, we're going to find your dresses. I want you to look as good as me. There will be no ugly bridesmaids in my pictures. Even though I'll be the focus, I can't have ugly invading my space," I told them both as we left the bridal shop.

"You ain't said nothing but a word," Charisse said with a laugh.

We had been in the shop for hours and I found all of my dresses and shoes in there. I was going to have my veil custom made and my jewelry would be coming from Harry Winston. I had hired one of the top wedding planning teams in the country to help me plan my wedding and it was going smooth so far. The brother-sister duo was more than happy to help when they realized that there was no budget for this over-the-top wedding. This was definitely about to go down as one of the most memorable events of the year.

Jason

I was sitting in my home office going over some paperwork getting more and more pissed by the second. I was looking over the budget for my latest project. It was a visual for Felicity's newest single. The director that we hired for the video had damn near tripled the projected cost and I was ready to peel his shit back. This shit was not what I signed up for. I was about to be broke before we made one dime off my woman. It didn't matter if I did or not, but this was Felicity's dream, and I wanted to make it happen for her.

"Why are you still in here? It's almost two in the morning," Felicity asked.

She must've woken up out of the coma I put her ass in earlier and come looking for me. She knew that I always made sure she was straight before I did any work at home. It was how we managed to have such a good balance lately. I was able to handle business in and out of the bedroom because she gave me the freedom to do so. She didn't get clingy or pissed that I had to take calls at all hours of the day and night, and I loved that about her.

"I'm trying to figure out why the fuck is this video costing me almost as much as one episode of *Post Wives*," I said. I damn near threw the papers in her direction.

"I guess it's because he wants to shoot the video in St. Thomas instead of Atlanta and then he wanted to add in a love interest for me," she stated, shoving the papers back at me.

"Fuck you mean a love interest? Ain't no other nigga putting his hands on you for a fucking video. Bad enough I let that bitch ass nigga touch all over you for this fuck ass show. I'm not with this shit at all," I said, letting my jealousy show once again.

"You know, I thought we had gotten past all of this when the shit with Dylan finally died down. But I see your ass still hasn't learned shit. I love your ass, and I only want your thick-headed ass," she spat.

"I'm just saying. This shit is just too much if you ask me. You need to get rid of one or both. I would much rather you get rid of this nigga they want all over you," I said with finality.

"And what about my co-star, who, by the way, is very gay? You want him gone, too? How the fuck can I have a career if you plan on blocking me from doing something that I love to do, and that's acting?" she fired back.

I just sat back and said nothing. I just stared off into space trying to figure out how just that fast we were sitting here arguing with each other. We went out to eat, saw a movie and then came back to my house and made love for hours. Now we were damn near screaming at each other.

"So, you're just going to sit there and act like I didn't say shit. Okay, my nigga, I can show you better than I can tell you," she said and stormed out of my office.

I sighed and rubbed my hands down my face. I knew I had fucked up by not saying anything, but I didn't know how to answer her questions. It was true that I hated the fact that she had to kiss and touch over her co-star. I knew that shit wouldn't come out of it, but it didn't mean that I had to like the shit one bit. I got up and ran up to my room to find Felicity packing all of the clothes she had left over in her duffel bag.

"Wait, what the fuck are you doing? I know you're not leaving," I said and tried to grab the bag from her.

The way she snatched the bag back from me had me shook. The amount of venom in her eyes caused me to stop dead in my tracks. I had never seen her look at me this way before, and I knew that I had royally fucked up. She was fed the fuck up with me, and I couldn't blame her at this point. All of my insecurities and jealousy pushed her to this point.

"Please, don't go. We can talk about it and work shit out," I pleaded with her.

"I don't have anything to work out. I'm secure enough in myself to trust you. It's just a fucking shame that I'm younger than you and I have more sense than you. You have bitches throwing their pussy at you all day every day, and do I trip? Fuck no. You know why? Because I know who I am and what I have to offer a nigga. And there ain't a bitch out there that can tell me otherwise," she stated.

"I get that. It's just you're so beautiful, and I," I couldn't even finish my sentence.

"You were the one keeping shit from me. I should have walked my ass away then, but no, my simple ass stayed because I saw you beyond all your street shit. But I refuse to deal with your jealousy. I won't let that turn into trying to control me and then that lead to some form of abuse. Get your shit together and I might be back. Until then, we can keep this shit professional," she said and then walked out my room.

I sat down on my bed and I felt tears stinging my eyes. I couldn't remember the last time my ass shed a tear. I didn't even cry at my dad's funeral, and that shit hit me hard as fuck. All I knew was that Felicity was the one for me and I couldn't for the life of me figure out why I couldn't get my shit together long enough to bury my insecurities.

I finally heard a door open and then close, and then a voice letting me know that my door had opened, closed and my alarm was set. Even pissed off at me, Felicity was still thinking of my safety by setting my alarm. I was going to do everything in my power to win my woman back. She was my wife, and I could feel it in my bones.

Felicity

J ason had me all the way fucked up. I was just trying to have my career and a life with him and only him, but his stupid ass couldn't see that shit. All I wanted to do was lay up with him and watch something on Netflix and eat a greasy ass pizza while Jason rubbed on my ass until I fell asleep. But of course, Mr. Control Freak wanted to act an ass about a nigga that I could give negative five fucks about.

I was so pissed off that I almost missed the turn to my street to go home. I made it back to my area in record time and I knew that Mama Gina would have questions on why I was coming home so late. I still couldn't believe that I broke up with Jason, but I did. I knew my worth and I refused to settle for anything less than the best.

I was so glad to see that the lights were out in the house and the porch light was still on. I clicked the key fob to disable the alarm from my car as I pulled up to the curb. I didn't want to pull into the driveway and alert Mama Gina that I was home. I was hoping that I would just wake up and see them in the morning. I just needed some time alone to get my thoughts and feelings together.

"What on earth are you doing here this time of night?" Mama Gina asked me as soon as I walked in the door, scaring the pure shit out of me.

"Too much to talk about right now. I just want to get some sleep and then talk to you after the sun comes up," I said wearily.

"It must be bad if you have to sleep on it. I know you, sugar, so I'll let you go on and get some rest. Avalon is staying with Ginger tonight," she explained.

"I figured because I saw Kenny's car out front. Y'all nasty," I joked.

"Shit, I'm grown and if I want to screw my man, I will," she shot back. I laughed hard as hell as I damn near sprinted to my room.

I almost lost my shit when I passed by Mama Gina's room and saw Kenny's whole bare ass standing up. I didn't think he knew I was in the house because he walked out of the room with his dick swinging. My eyes bucked at the sight of the baseball bat between his legs, and I knew right then why Mama Gina was so happy all the time.

"Aaah! Shit, maybe I need to go and get me a room," I exclaimed.

"My bad! I thought we were alone. I didn't know you came home," Kenny said as he tried to find something to cover up.

I quickly turned and went to my linen closet and tossed a towel over my shoulder. I didn't turn back around until he told me he was covered up. we just looked at each other and laughed. I felt like a kid that walked in on her parents instead of the grown woman that I was.

"What the hell is all that noise?" Mama Gina yelled as she came down the hall. When she saw me and Kenny laughing in the hallway, she started blushing.

"Uh-uh, don't try and hide now. You two up in here doing the freaky sneaky. I'm going to bed. Just don't leave a mess all over the house and try to keep it down. Oh, and no babies. I'm too old to be a big sister," I joked and ran to my room before Mama Gina could throw something at me.

I closed the door to my room and stood by the door for a moment. I heard the sounds of Najee start to play softly, and I knew that my mama was getting her back cracked again. I smiled to myself because even though my heart was breaking, I was so happy that Mama Gina had finally found love again. My phone chiming broke me from my thoughts.

I'm so sorry for what I put you through over the years. Hopefully you will be willing to come and visit with me so we can talk about our issues-Dylan.

I just looked at the message, leaving it on read. I didn't know if I should respond or not, so I left it alone for the time being. For some odd reason I felt like I was betraying Jason by even thinking about responding. Despite all the shit I talked earlier, my heart still was beating for that man. He was the one that made my mind go crazy and my heart stop whenever I was near him. I wanted him like no other, but I wasn't going to put up with whatever he had going on in his brain.

"I'm trying to protect my heart, but you're making it so hard. I guess it's safe to say you took my pain away."

Queen Naija's voice came through my phone. I looked down and saw that it was Ginger FaceTiming me. I steadied my racing heart because I thought that it was Jason and I didn't know if I would be able to stand my ground if he had called me right then. I sighed and plastered on a phony smile before I accepted the call.

"Bitch, why is your car outside? I thought that you were staying with your man," she asked.

"I broke up with him," I said with my voice shaking. I broke down in tears while I explained to her what happened.

"Aw, boo, I'm sorry. You know that I am here with ice cream and pizza any time you want to cry. But my bro needs to get his shit together before he loses out on the best thing that has ever happened to him," she said.

I told her that I was tired and wanted to get some sleep since it was almost four in the morning. I knew that Ginger would get Avalon off to school in the morning, and that was a blessing. It felt good knowing that I actually had a village to help raise my child. Ginger and I had worked out a system so that we could have time for our men and our kids while keeping our careers.

No one could tell us that we were bad mothers because we always knew where our kids were. If they weren't with us, they were with Mama Gina or doing something with Megan since her house was so big and she loved kids. I was so blessed to have friends like those two. I just wished that I had Jason at that moment because I knew that I wouldn't rest peacefully without him.

"OKAY, you need to get up. Your ass been asleep too long," I heard Mama Gina call out from my door.

She was glowing and smiling from all the dick she got last night. I couldn't wait to tell Ginger what I saw because that was an image that was seared dead in the center of my cornea for life. I just hoped and prayed that I never walked in on the two of them ever again.

"I'm coming, Ma. Is there any coffee?" I asked as I rubbed my eyes.

"You know I keep a pot brewing. Now get up, it's after one in the afternoon and Avalon will be home soon. Plus, you need to tell me what brought your ass home at three in the morning," she said as I followed her into the kitchen.

"Me and Jason broke up. I just can't deal with all of his hang ups and jealousy issues. I told him he needs to get it together and figure out what his deal is," I told her.

"Well, baby, all I can say is you know what you want to be so young. Now don't get me wrong, I love Jason, but jealousy can cause a lot of problems. I watch Oxygen and the ID channel," she said.

"I love him so much, Mama. That's why this hurts so much. I know if he calls me right now, I might go running back to him. That's why I'm not going into the studio today. I need a few days to get my strength up," I explained.

"Take your time, baby. If it didn't hurt, then I would question if you really did love him. But knowing how you're feeling lets me know that you really love that man and you didn't make this decision on an impulse," she advised.

"I know, Ma, I just don't get why he's so jealous. And I know that he's still hiding shit from me. I don't even know if I trust him at this point," I said and took a long sip of coffee.

"Just give it time. That's all the advice I have for you," she said. She fixed two cups of coffee and grabbed some pastries before heading back to the room with Kenny.

I picked up my phone and looked at the message from Dylan again. Something was telling me that it was a bad idea to respond, but a bigger part was saying that I needed to get closure and end that chapter of my life. Even if I never got back with Jason, Dylan needed to know that he and I could never be.

I will have one meeting with you. There better not be any bullshit behind this-Fefe.

No games, I swear. I promise you that I'm sober and doing better-Dylan.

Let me know when, where and what time, so I can make it happen-Fefe.

I put my phone down and wondered if I was making a mistake. Only time would tell.

Dylan

W hen I saw the text from Fefe, I wanted to jump for joy. I told her what she wanted to hear because the moment she sat down for my therapy session, I was going to confess all of my feelings for her. This time I would be sober doing it. I never thought that I would actually like being here, but I did. I had learned so much about myself and what triggered me to use.

"Hey, DJ, do you want to do some laps today?" Christina asked me.

"Yeah, I'll meet you in the pool in a half hour," I said.

Even though the physical attraction was there, Christina and I were just friends. She was really helping me get used to sober living. The first few days were the hardest while I was detoxing. I had two seizures, and one was so bad that they had to sedate me so that I wouldn't die.

It was the scariest moment of my life and the biggest wake-up call. I got my shit together quick, fast and in a hurry and started to take the program seriously. I thought that I would come here and get on methadone and just be cool. I wasn't serious at first, but now I couldn't wait to show the world the new, sober me.

"Hey, Dylan, before you go and work out, can I talk to you for a second?" Star asked me. I nodded and followed her to her office.

"You are becoming one of my best residents here. I mean, at first you fought the process and everything that we stood for. But I think your detox was the wake-up call you needed. I didn't want to tell you this and set you back, but we had to hospitalize you for a week. You were in a coma," she admitted.

I couldn't move. I thought that I just had a seizure and they had to sedate me. Star just sat here and told me that it was way more than that. She explained that they had to place me in a medically induced coma because the seizure that I had caused a massive amount of swelling in my brain. They had to perform a craniotomy to relieve the pressure and they weren't sure if I would ever wake up again.

"I feel so lucky. All the shit I was taking almost killed me because I felt guilty about letting my mom bully me into not being there for my daughter. I let the fact that I was only sixteen and I had a career cloud my judgement. I need to really apologize to Felicity and be a man for real," I said with a heavy sigh.

"That's one of the most important steps in your sobriety: asking for forgiveness and forgiving. You need to talk with your mother as well. You never know what was going on in her head to make her feel the way she did. Remember, she was raised in a different era," Star told me.

I just nodded my head and left out of her office. I had too much heavy shit loaded on me for one day. I went up to my room and changed into a pair of swimming trunks. I went down to the pool nearest to our side of the center and saw Christina stretched out on one of the lounge chairs.

I watched her skin look like it was dipped in chocolate crème. Her body looked as if it was made on the sixth day, because the Lord himself had to take a day off to admire it. I felt my dick start to stiffen up as I watched her from a distance. I didn't know what was going on, but I needed to get a handle on it and fast. I ran and dove straight in the water, making a huge splash.

"Boy! You scared the shit out of me. My heart went to my feet and then ran up my throat," Christina exclaimed.

"My bad, I thought you were up," I said.

"I fell asleep reading *In Love With the King of Harlem*. I laughed so hard when Tweeti told that girl to take the condom and run! I was weak as fuck," she said as she filled me in on the book she had started that morning.

"You get so involved with these books. Sometimes I think you're talking about real people," I said as I watched her ease herself into the water.

"Because they are in my mind. I can hear them, see them and even taste the food that they are eating. I don't know why, but books help me escape from the world and my problems for a while," she explained.

She suggested that I download the Kindle app to my phone and read the same book. Then we could have our own book club and talk about what we read. It sounded like a good idea and I told her that I would think about it and started swimming. We swam for about an hour before I got tired and decided to rest.

I decided to download the app and see what all of the hype was about. If it would keep my mind off my cravings and the urge to use, then I would do it. I created an account and downloaded the book and the next thing you know, I was all up in the book, just like Christina's ass. This girl was doing something to me that was changing my whole life, and I didn't know how to feel about it.

Felicity

"Come on, Fefe, I need you to get this one last run and then we can stop. Do you need a break?" Kente asked me.

"Yeah, I need like ten or fifteen," I said and stepped out of the booth.

We had been working on this one track for over three hours because I couldn't get my head in the game at all. This break up with Jason was throwing me off my game big time. I didn't know that it was going to affect me this way. I couldn't concentrate on anything because it seemed like no matter where I turned, he was there.

Like this morning. I showed up to the office at the ass crack of dawn after I dragged Kente out of Ginger's bed. They both wanted to beat my ass, but I couldn't care less. I wanted to be in the studio before Jason brought his ugly ass in the building. But my dumb ass was wrong as fuck.

As soon as Kente and I used our badges to gain entry in the building, there was Jason, looking like he had been living in the building. I knew that he probably could because he had a few small studio apartments on the top level for when filming took too long and people needed to get some rest. He even had a twenty-four-hour daycare that was open to anyone doing any type of business at his studios.

"Damn, Kente, she got you up and out before the roosters start up.

Felicity, what do you have planned for the day?" he asked the moment we came close to his personal space.

"Shit I plan to do," I snapped and walked off.

"I don't know what you did, my nigga, but damn. You better fix it and fix it fast before the next nigga do what you wouldn't," I heard Kente say.

I smiled and walked to the elevator so that I could get into the studio. That run-in was why my concentration was fucked up and I couldn't hit the notes the way I wanted to. I asked the son of a bitch ass nigga to give me some space, and his ass wanted to suffocate the fuck out of me with his presence. Then we had Raven's dumb ass wedding coming up in a couple of weeks that we promised to be at. Shit was all fucked up.

"Talk to me. I mean, first you wake me up during crack hoe hours of operation, just when I was about to slide in some pussy. Then, you damn near slit Jason's throat. And now you can't even hit a decent note, no offense," Kente said as I took a seat and grabbed a bottle of water.

"I broke up with him because his jealousy is getting to the point that I'm scared of what he will do next to keep his jealousy at bay. He doesn't want me to have a male love interest in a video that needs one. I can't kiss my co-star who is gayer than two fairies on ice skates in San Francisco during summer. So, tell me, what can I do?" I asked with tears sliding down my face.

"First, stop crying. No nigga is worth tears of pain. Next, you just work on you. Jason may be older, but his ass has a lot of growing up to do. He's used to women doing what he wants them to do. But with you, you have your own mind and demand that he be a man. It's scary and he doesn't know how to handle it," he explained.

"I mean, you have to look at things from his side. His wife left him for a younger guy. A guy that he had personally groomed himself. His trust was broken because of them and then you breeze into his life. Young, fresh and knowing exactly what she wants. Every man in America wants a piece of you. You're the new America's sweetheart and it scares him. So, he acts out and tries to protect what's his," Kente continued.

"I never thought about it that way," I said lowly.

"I know. You're still young, so sometimes you only see things one way. Now, let's get back to work," he said.

After that talk, I was ready to record five or six more songs. We knocked the song out thirty minutes later and Kente said that he could have it mixed and mastered in less than two hours because it was so perfect. I told him that I would see him later and decided that I was going to do a little retail therapy.

"Felicity, can we please talk?" Jason asked.

I turned around and really got a good look at him. Jason looked like he hadn't been getting any sleep. His beard had grown out and was in serious need of a shape up. His normal cut was looking raggedy and his suit needed to be pressed. If I didn't know him, I would have thought that he was smoking that shit.

"Two minutes, Jason. That's all I have for you. I have to get a dress for this circus we got invited to," I said.

"Cool. Can we talk in here?" he asked pointing to a conference room.

I followed behind him and prayed that no bullshit popped off. I had enough on my mind.

Jason

I was thanking the man upstairs for even allowing me to have two minutes to speak to Felicity. Since she walked out of my house weeks ago, I hadn't been able to sleep there. Everything about my house reminded me of her and I felt like I was being haunted by my stupidity.

Raven and the bullshit that she put me through made it hard for me to open up and trust a woman. It made it hard for me to believe that a woman could really love me for me and be with only me. I loved Felicity with everything in me, but I was scared that she would leave me the same way that Raven did. So, what did my dumb ass do? I lashed out and acted like a butt-hurt asshole.

"I'm sorry, Felicity. For everything that I put you through. I was dumb and I let what Raven did to me cloud my judgement," I started and then explained to her why I acted the way that I did.

"All you had to do was talk to me about your fears. I am very understanding, if you hadn't noticed. I accept your apology, but right now I need time to figure out if this relationship is worth it," she said.

She walked over to me and kissed me on the cheek before exiting the room. I just sat down in one of the chairs and put my head in my hands. I had to find a way to get my family back because it was killing me to just not have Felicity, but I missed the fuck out of Avalon, too.

That little girl wormed her way into my heart, and I loved her just like if she were my own child.

"You really need to get it together, son. You not gone win her back looking like a wolf," my mom said. "I saw Felicity leave out. I told her that I wanted to take Avalon and her friends to Disney next week."

"Ma, you need to stop trying to spoil that girl. Besides, I doubt Felicity will even let us spend time with Avalon," I sighed.

"Lies you tell. She just told me that we both are welcome to get Avalon whenever we want. She's not keeping us from that baby because you're retarded," my mom cracked.

"Well, damn, tell me how you really feel," I said with a smirk. Leave it up to my mom to make me smile when I wanted to punch a hole in the wall.

"Go upstairs and get yourself together. You look like a well-dressed meth head. And you smell like hot ass and garbage," she told me.

"Am I really that bad?" I asked and sniffed my armpits. Yeah, I was smelling like hot dog water and boiled onions. "Okay, I see your point. I'm heading to the top floor to get clean," I told my mom.

"Thank God! I thought I was going to have to take you outside and hose you down. After you get cleaned up, you're taking me to The Bridge for lunch. I want to try the pot de crème that *Food and Wine* magazine featured last month," she demanded.

I let her know that I would meet her there. "Make sure that they give us the chef's table and the house wine. And order me the lamb chops." I kissed my mom on the forehead and went to get pretty.

Three hours and a good shower later, I was looking like my old self. I left out of the studio apartment that I had been sleeping in and changed into a pair of Balmain jeans, a simple black polo shirt and a pair of crisp, white Air Forces. I didn't have any meetings lined up, so I figured that I would dress down for the day. I was also going to take a cue from Felicity and get myself suited and booted for this sham of a wedding.

I also needed to meet up with Ramon and warn him about Javad so that he could watch his back. I really didn't care for Raven, but no one deserved what was going to happen to her family. I knew for a fact that after the wedding, Javad and Raven's brother were planning on using the clout that came with the Negron name to try and get in with the Russian mob. This wasn't going to end well for anyone, and I didn't want to be caught up in any of it.

Raven

My wedding was just a few days away and I was getting more and more excited by the day. The entire time that I had been with Ramon I had fought, whined and complained because shit wasn't going the way I wanted it. I thought I was this boss ass bitch that could do and say what she wanted, but the day my dad knocked my ass out proved otherwise.

I was getting dressed in my suite of rooms and Ramon was down the hall in his. Even though we ripped each other's clothes off every chance we got, we still maintained separate rooms. But I hoped that would change once we got married. The dick he was serving me was on a whole other level and had me out here like a crackhead trying to get a bitch a fix every night.

"*Mi amor*, you look so beautiful. Don't put anything over that face," Ramon said from behind me.

"I hadn't planned on it, love. You know that today is my makeup trial. And the final fitting for my dress is right after. I was just happy that Ken's Magic Touch was able to squeeze me in so quickly. You're going to love me even more once you see me walk down that aisle," I gushed.

"I love you regardless. I only want to make my bride happy," he said as he kissed my bare shoulder.

"Well then, you know what to do," I stated, my eyes growing dark.

Despite the love that was growing for Ramon, I still had an axe to grind with Felicity. That bitch came in and shook everything in my life up. Where a softer bitch would just be happy and grateful that she found someone like Ramon, I wasn't that. When a bitch crossed me, I had to get that get-back. Felicity wasn't going to walk out of my wedding happy and on Jason's arm.

"It's all taken care of, love. Just relax and get ready to become a Negron," he softly assured me.

"When are we going to share the same bed? I mean, I know I complained about you being in here all the time at first, but I love you and I love lying next to you," I whined.

"We can as soon as you are pregnant with our first child. That has been the tradition in my family for ages. I have to be sure that you're in this for life. A child will bond us more than sex. When you are ready for that step, then we can live in the same rooms," he said and stood up.

"Why? Because you still want to fuck other bitches?" I asked.

"You don't question me about anything until you are my wife! You claim you love me, then give me a child. Prove it. If I fuck a bitch during my bachelor party, that's my right as a man. My last night as a bachelor, and damn right I will turn the fuck up. You just better make sure that pussy stays together, or I will kill your brother," he threatened.

My eyes bucked and filled with tears as I listened to how he spoke to me. Never in the entire time I had been held up with him had he raised his voice to anyone. I didn't recognize the man that I was looking at in the mirror. This was a monster and I wasn't sure about marrying him anymore.

"Look, I'm stressed out and I didn't mean anything I said. I'm not even having a bachelor party. But I am serious about the baby. In my family, things have always been that way. It is to ensure loyalty in both parties.

If the couple is serious about the commitment, then they can live apart until they have a baby. It took my parents five years, and neither ever stepped out on the other. I just want the same commitment," he explained.

I saw the stress lines on his face and knew that there was so much more that he wasn't saying. I didn't want to believe him, but when I saw the sincere look in his eyes, I knew that he was telling the truth. But it didn't mean that it was going to be that easy to get into my pants and good graces. Nope, I was about to break the bank with his ass.

"You know you have a lot of making up to do," I said with a smirk.

"I'll have the jet ready to fly to Beverly Hills. Rodeo Drive will never be the same again," he said as an apology.

I smiled and knew right then and there that this man was the one for me. With Jason, his apology consisted of throwing me a new purse or taking me on a cheap ass trip to Orlando. He never went out and did no shit like Ramon was doing.

This man made a mistake, verbally apologized and then tried to go above and beyond to make it up to me. Even though this was our first disagreement, he was making up for it in a major way. This was the shit that dreams were made of in my book.

I went to my closet and decided to change my clothes. I slipped on a pair of black ripped jeans that fit me like a second skin. I buttoned up a sky blue blouse and slid my feet into a pair of matching Louboutin's before grabbing my Celine bag and heading out to meet the driver. I had my hair and makeup trials and I wanted to be on time for once.

"OKAY, HUNTY, WHAT DO YOU THINK?" Mink, the makeup artist, asked me.

He spun me around at allowed me to look at myself in the mirror. I was absolutely flawless. My brows were micro-bladed to perfection and I looked like there was no foundation or powder on my face. My eyes were smoked out and the glitter was popping. My lips were lined, painted and glossed to look even more juicy and kissable than before.

"I love it, boo! Thank you so much. I want to fuck my own self," I exclaimed. There were some white women in the salon and their faces frowned up at my outburst.

"Don't pay those bitches no mind. They just mad 'cause the dicks they got at home don't work," he whispered in my ear.

I giggled and just continued to look at myself in the mirror. I looked fine as fuck and there wasn't a soul out there that could tell me different. I wanted to show Ramon, but since this was the look that I was going to use for the wedding, he wouldn't be able to see it.

"Well, I love this look, bitch. I can't wait until you do this at my wedding. I'll pay you triple your fee to be available the whole day for touch ups," I said and handed him a stack of money.

"Shit, you just paid my booth rent for the year. A bitch about to make bank," he said and started twerking.

I laughed hard as fuck. I asked him to remove my wedding face and give me something fit for shopping in Beverly Hills. I knew that the paparazzi stayed posted up out there, and I wanted to look my best. I had to make sure that the world knew that I wasn't still hung up on Jason. I wanted the world to know that I was with a man that loved me and only me.

Dylan

"Dylan, you have a visitor," Star said into the phone that was in my room.

"I'll be down in just a second," I said and then hung up.

I jumped up fast as hell and made sure that I looked right. My hair was freshly cut, and I had been growing out my beard. I looked older and sexier, if I do say so myself. I pulled on a pair of black joggers and a fitted, white t-shirt. I slid my feet into a pair of Gucci sneakers and sprayed on some Tom Ford cologne.

Felicity let me know that she was in Miami doing an appearance and would come and see me while she was in Florida. I hadn't seen my baby momma in weeks, and I was itching just to look in her eyes. I saw that she and Jason were having issues in the blogs, but I didn't know how true it was.

"Hey, Dylan. You look good," she admired when I got close to her.

"You look beautiful as always," I said and pulled her in a hug. I was shocked that she returned the hug and didn't slap me. But I figured that she was being polite because of the fact that I was in rehab.

"Let's go out by one of the pools and sit," I said and led the way to the pool that had a view of the blue waters of the ocean.

"This looks like a resort, not rehab. You sure you're not on vacation and telling me some bullshit?" Felicity questioned after she sat down on one of the lounge chairs.

"I'm sure. Shit, my ass went through withdrawals so bad I almost didn't make it. I've been sober for sixty days now. I have another month here and then I move into a sober living house in Atlanta. I want to get my career back and finally be a real father to Avalon," I explained.

"That's great! I really am proud of you, Dylan. You were a good guy once. That's why I was crushing on you so hard back then," she admitted to me.

For a while we sat and just reminisced about Hollywood and how far we came from the kids that used to sneak kisses in between studios. It felt good to just talk to Felicity and see that she was really a great woman. Even though I had ulterior motives for coming to rehab at first, I realized that I had grown up a lot.

I wasn't thinking about romantically pursuing Fefe. I wanted to just be her friend and co-parent with her the best way I knew how. She didn't deserve any of the hell I put her through in the past and recently. I was the one that turned her life upside down every chance I got, and that shit wasn't cool.

"Look, ever since I got here, I fought everything that they were telling me. I wanted to break you and Jason up, but not for the right reasons. I wanted to piss off my mom, and to prove to Jason that I could take his bitch again. No offense," I said.

"None taken. I mean, I knew there was some shit with you when you decided to pop back up in my life after eight years of silence. Plus, you had Raven in your ear. That bitch has a forked tongue and sucked your dick with it every night," she spat.

"Trust and believe, I know exactly what you mean. We stayed high on something and she was able to get in my head easier. She used Avalon and the love I have for you to play all of us. I just hope she's getting her life together," I told Felicity.

"Well, we will see at this bougie ass wedding she invited me and Jason to. This shit is about to be a circus," she said and laughed.

I still couldn't believe that Raven managed to get another sucker to put a ring on it. I was almost one of them. I really thought the bitch loved my ass. I was with her for four fucking years and all she did was whine, bitch, moan, complain and anything to drive me to get higher than normal to drown out her voice.

She was always talking about Jason and what he would or wouldn't do for her. When he wasn't jumping at her demands, she would become this monster until I let her snort up a few lines of whatever pill I crushed up. Our entire relationship was back and forth, up and down, and now I was glad that part of my life was finally over. I wished Raven nothing but the best, but I needed her to just be a memory in my head.

I focused back on Felicity and the stories she was telling me about our daughter. Our little Avalon was growing into such a beautiful girl and I wish I could say that I had a part in it, but the sad fact of reality was that I didn't do shit but knock her mom up and run. I was trying to make up for it now by getting my shit together. I just hoped that I wasn't too late to have my chance to be a father.

"She definitely has your attitude, Fefe. You were the same way back in the day. You would say off the wall shit and then look at us like we were the ones that said it," I said as I cracked on her.

"Because those people rode the short bus as kids. Not my fault they didn't know their right from the right-right," she joked back.

"I'm glad I came out here today. You're doing so well, and I am really proud of you," she observed.

"I'm glad you did, too. I didn't think that Jason would allow you to come," I admitted.

"That's because we're taking a break. I couldn't deal with his jealousy issues. He needs to figure out what he really wants out of life. He also needs to figure out if I am the woman that he can be with. I am not some weak ass bitch that is willing to let him dictate my life," she stated.

"That's fucked up on his end. I know you're a good ass woman. If I had any sense, I would have made you mine and helped you raise Avalon from day one. But our time was then," I told her wistfully.

"That was what I was trying to tell your big-headed ass. I'm so happy that you understand that. Now we can finally be friends and co-parent like we were meant to do," she said.

I asked her more about her and Jason after that. She told me that if they were meant to be, then they would be. Until then, she was going to enjoy her life and not make any excuses as to why she was doing what she was doing. She was now living her best life and it was showing from the Fendi boots on her feet, to the Prada blouse that was hugging her breasts like a second skin.

"Since I can sleep knowing that you're not plotting on getting me back, can I give you a bit of advice?" she asked me.

"Sure," I said.

"Take it slow with her. You're both healing from something, so don't rush things. Something tells me that she's good for you," she said and glanced over at Christina.

I had been stealing looks at her the whole time that Felicity visited with me. I didn't think that Felicity noticed, but she was more observant than I gave her credit for. She noticed the growing attraction that I had for Christina, even though I had been fighting my feelings for her since I had been in this place. I thought that Felicity was who I was supposed to be with, but maybe she was just supposed to be the best friend that she started out being ten years ago when we were kids. Only time would tell.

Felicity

I was finally back home and getting dressed at Jason's condo for Raven's wedding. Since I got back from Miami, I had been able to be cordial with Jason. I wasn't snapping at him anymore, so that was progress. We also had managed to sit in a meeting about where they wanted my character on the show to go. I loved that they were allowing my character to evolve into someone amazing.

I was so happy that all of my hard work was paying off. I was proving to the world, not only myself, that I didn't need Jason or his clout to be successful. I could make my career pop all on my own. I was strong as fuck and I didn't need no nigga to prop my ass up. I could do that with the walls in my house or a chair that I bought.

"You look fine as fuck," Jason said while I zipped myself up in my dress.

I was sliding into a taupe, beaded Diane von Furstenberg designer original dress. It was made of raw silk and hugged my body like a glove. I matched the dress with a pair of nude YSL pumps and gold jewelry. My hair was swept up in an elegant bun high on my head, showing off a pair of chandelier earrings that Jason bought me for tonight.

"You don't look so bad yourself," I said as I admired him.

Jason was wearing an Armani suit the same color as my dress. He was wearing a pair of cream-colored Armani loafers and his gold Rolex. I walked over to him and helped him secure his gold and diamond cuff-links. I caught a whiff of his Creed cologne and felt my kitty purr.

"I want to bend your ass over right now," he whispered in my ear. A shiver went up my spine when he said that.

I shouldn't have been so weak for this man, but I needed some dick. I was feeling like Summer Walker because this girl needed some love. I did get my nut off the night before when Jason ate my pussy like he hadn't had a meal in a year, but that just left my ass wanting him to slide his dick between my walls. I was horny and a vibrator could only do so much.

"You play too much. You know that we are only going as friends," I said backing up from him.

"Oh, word. You weren't hollering that we were friends when my face was swimming in that wet ass pussy last night," he reminded me.

I couldn't say anything while my face turned red from embarrassment. I wanted to say something back, but Jason gave me this sexy ass smirk that I wanted to kiss. I was so glad that the car service called and let us know that the limo that Jason hired for the evening was waiting for us. He handed me my gold clutch and then we were out of the door.

"You two look ready to paint the town," the doorman said when we entered the lobby.

I smiled while Jason handed the man a five-hundred-dollar tip. When I asked him why he did that, Jason told me that the older man was working to pay for an experimental drug trial to help with his wife's Huntington's disease. I saw a different side of Jason in that moment. It was something that he never shared with me in all of the time that we had known each other.

Jason was a man who had a big heart and that made him even more attractive to me. It was so hard for me to not fall right back into his arms. I really wanted Jason to understand that I meant every word that I said the night I walked out on him. I was standing my ground and he needed to know that I wasn't the kind of woman that would fall right back after an earth-shattering orgasm.

"You know I'm going to fuck you back here after the wedding. I want to hear you scream while the city passes on by," Jason said.

"You really need to stop. We will not relive the drama that was our relationship," I said while sipping on the champagne that was in the back of the limo.

"Well, I want everything back. The drama, the smiles, Avalon, even Ginger and the girls. I miss all of you," he said, melting my heart.

"I really don't know, Jason. I don't think that I could set myself up for failure like that again," I admitted, revealing my fear.

"I understand all of that. But I really do need you in my life. I don't think that I can do any of this without you. Felicity, you are the reason that I wake up in the morning. Even when you cuss me out, I smile because it shows that you still care. I know that I'm not perfect, and I let my insecurities run you away, but I am going to run beside you until you give me another chance," he said.

With a declaration like that, who could resist? This man knew exactly what to say to make my walls come crumbling down. He was everything that I had been looking for in a man, with the exception of his jealousy. While I wanted Jason back in the worst way, I didn't want to blindly walk back into a relationship full of accusations and jealousy. Jason was going to have to jump through hoops and run a marathon to get back in my good graces.

"You have to work for this. If you think I'm worth it, you'll do whatever it takes to make me happy," I demanded.

"Anything you ask, I'll do it," he said.

"First, kiss me," I said. I was glad that I wore my smudge-proof makeup, because the way that Jason pounced on me would have sent my regular lipstick all over my face. I felt that kiss all the way back to my childhood and then five years in the future.

"That's a start," I managed to croak out after we pulled apart.

"I bet." He smirked.

While I was recovering from the kiss, I noticed that we had made it to Ramon's compound where the wedding was taking place. I was in awe of the massive size of the place. It looked like it was never-ending, like the rabbit hole in *Alice in Wonderland*. You probably needed a map and a guide to just to find a bathroom.

"Well, damn. Who knew this bitch was living like this?" I said as the door to the limo opened, and we were looking at the most beautiful rose garden I had ever laid my eyes on.

There were actual gold chairs lined up on each side of an aisle that was encrusted with Swarovski crystals. At the end of every other row, there were six-foot tall vases filled with the whitest roses I had ever seen. Each rose had a diamond in the center of it. There was a four-string quartet playing softly and a wait staff floating around with flutes of champagne and trays filled with different types of amuse bouche.

I grabbed a glass of champagne and a petit four and found a seat on the bride's side of the garden. I felt out of place as I watched some of the most powerful men in the world walk around with these women on their arms who looked like they slept in diamonds. I was just a struggling actress trying to live her dreams. These were all kept women who probably had never lifted a manicured finger to do anything but swipe a credit card.

"You look like a virgin in a prison cafeteria," a woman said as she sat down beside me.

"I am a little nervous. This is a little out of my league," I admitted.

"Don't be intimidated by the women. Most of them are blind to the fact that their husbands are sleeping with the bridesmaids," she whispered, causing me to choke.

"How do you know all of this?" I had to ask.

"My sister is in the bridal party and is sleeping with that man over there. She is his exclusive mistress. He only brings his wife out for big events like this. Other than that, you always see my sister on his arm. I hate it, but she loves it. By the way, I'm Peach." The woman extended her hand and I placed mine in hers.

"Ouch!" I exclaimed when her ring pinched my hand.

"I'm so sorry. I need to get the prongs fixed on this thing," she said smugly.

I got this weird feeling suddenly and felt the need to be near Jason. I turned my head for a moment to see if I could spot him. I saw him standing with a man who looked like a masculine form of Raven. He was older with a touch of gray peppering his hair, but he still looked young.

I turned back around and finished my champagne. I told Peach that I would talk to her at the reception and went to stand with my man. For some reason, I needed to be close to him. Something just started to feel off about the whole place and I had no idea what it was. I just hoped it was my mind playing tricks on me.

Raven

My wedding day was finally here. I was so excited as I sat in my suite of rooms getting pampered. The day started off with breakfast in bed served by Wolfgang Puck's latest mentee. Ramon had a masseur come up and give me a hot stone massage to prepare me for the day.

"Everyone is here and in place," the wedding planner said after my massage.

I wasn't worried about the staff or the guests. I was only worried about walking down the aisle and getting my revenge. Ramon had his friend's mistress, Peach, in place to help me exact my revenge. She was going to be the one to drug Felicity so that it would be easy to get her away from Jason.

I strategically placed Peach at the table with Jason and Felicity, so that when Felicity started to show signs of being too drunk, Peach would be able to get her away. Ramon and I had this all planned out and I was sure this was going to work.

"Time to get in that beautiful gown," Naima said.

I had formed some sort of friendship with her over the months and it was safe to say that she was the one bridesmaid who was always available to me. She helped me so much during the planning of the wedding. I felt somewhat bad for how I treated her when the cameras weren't rolling on us. And for snatching Jason from her. But that was only for a moment.

I really just wanted to show everyone that I was the one that came up on top. There was nothing that anyone could do to take me down. I was that bitch and now everyone in the world was about to know it. I let out a self-satisfied sigh and stood up from my seat on my bed.

I dropped my robe, unashamed of my nakedness, and slid into the La Perla set that I had set out for the day. Naima and the seven other bridesmaids helped me into my corset and slip. I wrapped my robe back around me and sat in a chair while my glam squad filed in to make me beautiful.

Three hours after I sat down, I was sliding into the dress that I was going to walk down the aisle in. I stepped into the diamond-crusted Louboutin's and then Naima placed the veil on my head. I looked at myself in the mirror and had to do a double take. I was shocked at how beautiful I looked, and I was a confident woman already.

"Let's get you married," Naima whispered.

I took a breath and left my room for the last time as a single woman. I walked out of the room towards the elevator that led to the back of the compound. I could see the décor from the double-sided glass enclosure that I had Ramon put in. I loved fucking him in the elevator and looking out at the garden. Now I was watching my Rose Diamond-themed wedding take place on the way down.

The butterflies started to move in my belly the closer we got to the bottom floor. Naima stepped out before me into the conservatory where the rest of my bridesmaids were waiting. The gasps and sighs from the women boosted my already over-inflated ego. I grabbed my bouquet of diamond-filled roses and ordered everyone to line up.

Ohh, ohhh,

I crave...

I wake up to shadows

touching your pillows, looking for a trace of you smile.

And that's when it hit me, you're no longer with me

in fact it's been quite a while

Since I sit here drinking coffee as you sipped your tea.

And you swore you'd always love and always care for me

And even though there's no more else to save...

It's you I crave

I crave your touch

I crave your lips

I miss so much

the excitement of you kiss

But since your gone my heart won't behave

MARC DORSEY CAME out and started to sing my favorite song while my bridal party started their stroll down the aisle. When I saw Naima finally take her place, Damiana, the wedding planner, opened the doors and then I stepped out so my dad could take my hand and lead me to my husband.

The ceremony was beautiful, and everything went perfectly. The kiss that Ramon laid on me let me know that he was going to fuck me senseless later that night. We drove to the other side of the compound where there were huge tents set up so that we could eat, dance and drink the night away. We hired the biggest chefs and entertainers to make sure everyone had a good time.

Ramon came out of his pockets for this wedding. I knew he spent at least ten million dollars on the ceremony alone. But it was all worth it in the end because I got the man of my dreams and he had the baddest bitch on his arm. I had changed into the dress that I was wearing for entering the reception for our first dance.

It was an all-lace House of Chappelle original that was tight and flared out at the bottom. It showed the right amount of cleavage and sparkled with hand-sewn crystals. I matched it with a pair of Alexander McQueen heels and my wedding ring alone was enough bling. Ramon blessed me with a twenty-five carat, radiant cut diamond in a platinum and diamond setting.

"Congratulations, Raven. You look amazing," I heard Felicity's annoying ass voice say as some of the guests came up to us to give congratulations.

"Thank you. You're looking healthier. You don't have any news for us?" I asked snidely while making a gesture suggesting she was pregnant.

"Not this time. This is just happy weight. I'm not ashamed to be thick. It suits me." She smiled, making me want to vomit.

"Well, it's working for you. I hope you and Jason have a good time tonight," I remarked snidely.

"I hope so, too. Everything is so gorgeous. You really know how to plan a party. This is your calling. I would love to talk to you if you can get away from your groom," she said.

I was taken aback by her friendly demeanor. I mean, I meant this girl the biggest harm, and here she was being really nice to me. I looked up at Ramon, and he gave me a small nod and smile, letting me know it was okay to go and talk. He kissed me softly on the lips and I walked off with Felicity.

"Look, I know you hate me and all that I stand for, but look at all of this. This man gave you a multi-million-dollar wedding. This is something that girls like me can only dream of. I just wanted to tell you that despite it all, I really am happy that you found your Prince Charming," she said, laying it on thick.

"Who knew your ass could be so poetic?" I managed to weakly reply.

"Don't tell me you have a soft side and are crying?" she joked.

I realized that she was right and felt soft tears on my face. Thank goodness for the power of setting spray. My makeup was smudge-proof and I was so grateful in that moment. I knew then that I couldn't go through with my plan because I saw why Jason loved her so much.

Felicity was just a beautiful soul and you could almost touch her energy. I was the fucked up one. I was a spoiled ass bitch that didn't like to lose for shit. I was wrong as fuck and now I had to find a way to call this whole shit off before it went too far. I had to do better if I wanted to live better.

"Well, let me apologize for being a stank ass bitch. I was high as fuck most of the time and that triggered my anger to do dumb shit. I wanted to make you suffer because I was jealous of you," I admitted to her.

We stood and talked about my insecurities and how I grew up. Felicity never once judged me or looked at me different. In fact, she gave me the best advice and told me to stop letting men run my life. I needed to do what made me happy, and that was live for me regardless of who liked it. It was great advice from someone so young, and I planned on using it.

"Let me let you get back to your husband, and I'm going to hit the bar up since the liquor is paid for," she joked and walked off.

"Now, that wasn't so hard was it?" I heard Ramon say from behind me.

"It really wasn't, baby. I actually feel free," I said and wrapped my arms around his neck and started to slow dance with him.

I got lost in Ramon's eyes as he looked down on me. There was nothing but love and admiration in his eyes for me, and I realized that I could have lost it all in my plot for revenge. I was sure that if I decided to have Felicity snatched up, Jason wouldn't hesitate to kill my husband. I would be a widow before my honeymoon.

When the song ended, we parted ways and my father stepped in for the father-daughter dance. Even though we had a difficult relationship, I was so happy that he showed up for my day. When I married Jason, he refused to come, and I felt like that was the beginning of the end of my first marriage. It was one of the biggest roadblocks throughout my entire relationship with Jason.

"Daddy, I'm so happy you walked me down the aisle. Your blessing means the world to me," I gushed.

"I shouldn't have taken this long. You should have married him when I told you and then we wouldn't have to go through all of this," he grumbled.

"Damn, Daddy, you can't just be happy for me. You always have to fuck up a moment," I pouted. "And what do you mean, 'go through all of this'?" I asked.

"Just know that you can't stop a boulder once it starts rolling down the mountain," he said.

I knew then that my night was going to do a complete one-eighty right into Hell.

Jason

The wedding was actually nice. I was nervous that Raven would be up to her old tricks, but Felicity told me that they actually had a good talk and that they managed to bury the hatchet in the ground and not in each other's lace fronts. That was a good thing because Ramon had let me in on what Raven had planned for Felicity. She just didn't know that my girl saved her life.

But looking at Raven dance with Javad, I knew that something was wrong. My senses went into overdrive while I searched for Felicity with my eyes. When I couldn't locate her, I started to panic. I took off searching each tent for her. I couldn't find her among the crowds of people, so I looked for Ramon.

I saw him standing with the mayor of Atlanta and the police commissioner having a conversation. I walked over to him with my hands shaking. I knew in my heart that something happened to Felicity. There was just a feeling that came over me telling me that she needed me. I just didn't know where to find her.

"Gentlemen, I'm sorry to interrupt, but I need to talk to the man of the hour for a second," I said faking joy.

"What's wrong? I can see it in your eyes, my friend," Ramon asked as soon as we were out of the range of the guests.

"Something isn't right. I can't find Felicity, and Javad has your wife over there looking like someone just shit on her shoes. It's time to squad up," I said.

We snuck off into one of the garden houses that was actually one of the security posts to look at the footage of the reception. This nigga had more security than the White House and Buckingham Palace combined. The picture was so clear that you could see the bumps on the tongues of the people talking. He also had crystal clear sound, so we could hear everything going on.

While looking at the footage, I saw something that made my blood boil. I saw Javad talking to the beautiful woman that Felicity was talking to prior to the wedding ceremony. He handed her a small vial and she kissed him on the lips. They both had these smirks on their faces like they were up to something. We went forward a little more and then I saw the same woman helping Felicity into the main house.

Felicity looked like she was drunk off her ass which wasn't like her at all. She rarely drank, and when she did, she only had two glasses of whatever she was having. She didn't like how she felt the last time she got drunk in public, and only drank more than two drinks when she was at home. She said that she always wanted to be in control when she was out in public because the press was always watching.

"Who the fuck is that bitch?" I roared.

"That's Peach. Her sister was in the wedding. I don't know who she came with, but I'm guessing it was Javad. I hope he didn't do what I think he did," Ramon said.

Ramon rubbed his hand across his face and let out a frustrated breath. When I got a look at his face, all I saw was rage in his eyes. He got roped into Javad's bullshit and now there was about to be a massacre in his home. We knew that we had work to do if we wanted to find Felicity before they were able to make it off the premises and we lost track of them.

"Tell security we have a Melina situation," Ramon said. I remembered his mom was taken from their home in Colombia during his parents' anniversary party. It was the main reason why he had the security he did.

"Go out there and act normal. I don't want to alert Javad or make Raven feel bad. I want her to remember her wedding as the happiest moment of her life. I really do love that woman. I have, since the first day I met her," Ramon stated.

"I loved her at one point myself. But Felicity is my one. I will burn the whole city to the ground if she's not back in my arms tonight!" I yelled.

"We will get her back, my friend. And then we will deal with Javad. He's crossed the wrong man," Ramon tried to reassure me.

I didn't say anything else. I turned on my heels and left out of the security room and went back to the party. It looked like it was in full swing and Raven had changed again into a lace jumpsuit. She looked so happy and I couldn't help but smile a little as I thought back to our wedding day. She smiled that day, but it wasn't anything like the smile that was on her face this day.

"You need to find your woman and dance," Raven slurred as she walked up to me.

She had to be drunk if she was coming to me like she was. We were anything but friends, and I think that she forgot that in that moment. But I remembered Ramon's warning, so I was going to entertain my ex-wife, his new wife, for a moment. This was her day, and I refused to bring drama like she was trying to at one point.

"I like her, Jay. She's not me, which says a lot about her. But you know what? We shouldn't have ever gotten married. I took you from Naima because they gave her my prize. I was just a jealous ass bitch and I had to stop her ass from winning out every time. I was dumb and high. But I still won," she admitted.

"You did win. You're married to a good man. Don't let anyone fuck it up for you," I cautioned.

"Trust me, I won't. Ooh, that's my shit!" she yelled when she heard Megan Thee Stallion's "Cash Shit" playing. She ran off from me and started twerking on the dance floor.

"It's fucked up that I have to kill her father. But this pussy brought it on himself," Ramon said as he walked up next to me.

"Have they found them yet?" I asked. My trigger fingers on both hands started to itch. That meant that someone had to die, and soon.

Felicity

My head was throbbing, and my throat felt like I ate a dozen Popeyes biscuits without water. My stomach was doing a familiar dance and I knew what was about to happen next. I leaned over and released the contents of my stomach. I heard my vomit hit the floor and echo off the walls making me want to throw up all over again.

I didn't know where I was. All I knew was that it was dark, and I was naked and freezing. Someone had to have slipped something in my drink because there was no way that I would have let myself get caught out there like that. After years in the military, I was painfully aware of my surroundings at all times. But I let my guard down to have fun, and now I was paying the price.

"Shit, she's up. This cannot happen. Not now. We have to move her fast. We cannot risk getting caught," I heard a man say.

"You're going to get us killed! This is stupid. I knew I should have never went along with your plan. Now my family will die!" I heard a familiar voice whisper sharply.

"Ugh! Aah!" I cried out before throwing up again. At this point, I had nothing left in me but sour tasting stomach acid coming out, and it was disgusting. It made me vomit all over again.

"This isn't right. She shouldn't be reacting like this. What did you give her?" I heard the man ask again.

I managed to pick my head up and regretted that decision. It felt like all of the defensive backs of a division one college football team were jumping on my temples. Then the moment I opened my eyes, the room looked like I was under water. But I managed to see who was talking.

It was the woman Peach that I had spoken to before the ceremony and Raven's father. I should have known that Raven's bitch ass had something to do with this. This had her stank ass pussy smeared all over it. I couldn't wait to get away from these two so that I could get back to my daughter.

"All I gave her was a molly. How the fuck could I know that the bitch couldn't handle a fucking pill? She's as weak as your dumb ass daughter. I saw her being all friendly with the bitch that took her man and your security. You knew that as long as she was at least speaking to Jason that the Russians wouldn't touch you. But she married Ramon, and now all bets are off. You crossed the Colombians and then double-crossed the Russians. They will kill us all!" she admitted.

I just laid there listening to the entire conversation realizing why Raven was as twisted as she was. It wasn't her fault at all. Her father was the sickest man that I had ever laid eyes on. He tried to pimp his daughter out to the highest bidder for years and had even arranged for Raven to marry Ramon when she was seventeen, all so he could have money to spend and rob other people.

This man was sicker than what you could find in an urban novel, but I guess that was why they said truth was stranger than fiction. I had to find a way to get in contact with Jason. Someone had to warn him, Raven and Ramon that the Russians were on the warpath and that Javad had fired the first cannon. I just had to be smart.

"We have to give her something, so she doesn't die. We need her alive as a bargaining tool. We get the money, pay the Russians back and then we go back to my homeland where we can get lost in the crowds of people. It's perfect. Plus, they won't figure out it was us. Go back to the party and act like nothing is wrong. When they ask you about this bitch, tell them that you helped her to the bathroom and that was the last time you saw her, or some shit," he instructed.

"I can't do that. You know that they will know I'm lying," she pleaded.

"You're going to do what the fuck I said!" he roared and slapped Peach.

She ran out of the room with the quickness and I had a moment of relief followed by dread. The look that Raven's father gave me sent chills down my spine. It was like he was fucking me with his eyes. I wished now that Peach hadn't left me alone with this man. I couldn't defend myself because I was so weak from the molly they slipped in my drink.

"You don't have to worry about me touching you. You are way too young for me, even though you are a very desirable woman. I can see why men are going crazy over you," he said and licked his lips seductively. If I had anything left in me, I would have let it go all over him.

"You're dead once Jason finds out it was you," I weakly spat.

"As you kids say, but the gag is, he won't. At least not until I'm far away from you. Once Peach delivers you back to them, she'll pay with her life, not me," he stated proudly.

"And what about your kids? Did you even think about them?" I asked. I just had to know more about what kind of men my father and Javad were to not give a shit about the people that came from their own nuts.

"You think that my family gave a damn about me when I married their mother? I was written off the wills because I chose love. Then the kids came, and my father loved them. They get MY money! They don't deserve it, I do!" he yelled.

This man sold out his kids for money that he wasn't entitled to? While

I agreed that it was wrong to cut off a child because of who they loved, it still didn't excuse the hatred and greed in his heart. If Jason didn't kill him, I would, just because he reminded me of my father.

I just prayed that Jason found me before I had to do something that I thought I would never have to do in my life: take another man's life.

Jason

I went to my basement to have some fun. I didn't tell the guys, but I had someone who would tell me everything I needed to know. I just had to let them sit long enough to run their mouth.

I opened the door and flicked on the lights to reveal Peach hanging upside down from a beam in the ceiling. I knew that she was in on Felicity's disappearance. The way she was acting the night of Ramon and Raven's wedding put me on high alert. She was shifting around and stuttering every time we asked her about Felicity and her taking her to the bathroom. She was just moving way too funny for me.

"Oh my god, my head!" she screamed when I entered the soundproof room.

I gave a sadistic laugh as I approached her. She was a beautiful woman, that was very evident. But there was something dead in her beyond the surface beauty. She was soulless and it unnerved me just a bit. I didn't know how to take her and the flip way she acted about Felicity being missing.

"You think I give a flying fuck about your got damned head? You need to tell me where the fuck my girl is before your head gets sent to your mom and your body to your sister. Let them put you together for your funeral, bitch!" I spat.

"I don't know where she is. I told you that already," she whined.

I didn't believe a word that came out of her mouth, so I did what I did best when I was backed up against a wall; snap. I pulled a thick leather belt from a hook on the wall and began to mercilessly beat Peach until she passed out. I let her rest for thirty minutes before taking her down from the hooks and strapping her to the metal table that I found when a slaughterhouse was being auctioned off.

I knew that my contractor thought I was touched as fuck in the head when I had him renovate this room like this. He probably thought I was into some sick sexual shit. I mean, I was into some freaky shit, but this was to satisfy my need to hurt someone when the need arose.

I tossed some water on Peach's face to wake her dumb ass up. She screamed out in pain when she realized that she was sitting in saltwater. I knew that what I was doing was sick and tortuous, but this was the only thing that I could think of to get the answers I needed.

"You're a sick ass bastard! You'll never find her. If you don't pay the money, no one will see your sweet Felicity again," she cackled.

My anger reached such a fever pitch that I forgot she was a woman and punched her so hard in the face that I felt her teeth shatter. Blood shot from her mouth and onto my shirt, but I didn't give a shit that she ruined my seven-hundred-dollar shirt. I just wanted the information that I knew she had.

"If I don't show up, she won't be found again. You have no idea how sick that bastard really is," she cried.

I guess she figured that the beating would continue, and she didn't want to suffer any more. But what she revealed to me sent a chill through my body. I knew that Javad was into some sick shit, but I needed to know what Felicity was facing and how much time I had left.

"You better open your dick suckers and let them shits fly. I don't have all day," I growled.

"Just don't kill me. If you do, she will disappear," she pleaded and warned.

"No promises. I want all the information. Even something as small as the brand of sugar he puts in his coffee," I told her and then sat back and waited for her to talk.

"Javad got into the sex trade years ago. Raven was supposed to be his first sale, but then he thought that by marrying her off into the Negron family he would be safe. But Raven had other plans for her life. Then when she married you and he found out who your father was, he made even more moves in the sex trade. He thought that your name bought him time, but all he did was piss off the Russians, Colombians and Haitians.

"Now he owes the Russians nearly a million dollars and he is desperate as hell and is pulling out all of the stops so that he can live. I bet that he's even willing to sell Felicity. He knows that Raven is untouchable because of Ramon, but Fefe is fair game."

She told me how Javad had pretty much ran through all of his money and ended up borrowing from the Russians to pay off the Haitians. And when he couldn't pay the Russians back, he had to do something. That's why when he found out about Raven's plan to snatch Felicity, he went along with it.

"So, where is he?" I asked.

"The old stables on the other side of the lake," she confessed before passing out again.

I sat back and lit another blunt while thinking. All this time she had been right there under our noses. There was no telling what she was going through or if she was still even there. But this could have been all avoided if Peach's dumb ass had said something the moment we asked her. Now I had to kill two people and possibly pay off people that I hadn't dealt with in years.

"Mikael, my friend. We need to talk. Are you still in town?" I asked the young Russian when he answered.

"Ah! Jason, I am. Come to my hotel. I am at the W. We will drink and talk. One hour," he said in his broken English.

I tossed a thin blanket on Peach and locked her back in the room. I left her with a sandwich and water before I locked her in. I was a lot of things, but I wasn't a complete asshole. I needed for her to keep her strength up. Peach didn't know it, but she was going to be the key in bringing Javad down for good.

I climbed into the Lamborghini that I planned on giving to Felicity for her birthday that was in a few weeks. I needed to get downtown fast and this car was the fastest in my garage. My other car was still at my condo and I didn't feel like having someone bring it to me.

I pulled up to the hotel and had the valet park my car for me. I saw the upper class people walking in and out of the building, not paying me any attention. I walked to the elevator and got on. I pushed the button for the floor that Mikael told me that he would be on and waited while the elevator ascended. I reached the floor, got off the elevator and then walked towards his room. When he opened the door after I knocked, he pulled me into a huge bear hug like he always did.

"Jason! So good to see you. You look like father did. Ah, to be young again," the older man said to me.

No one knew Mikael's real age. We all just knew that he had been in the game for over thirty years. He and my father had a great business relationship, but Mikael was into more than just drugs. He had his hand in oil, guns, sex and whatever else you could name.

"Thanks, my man. But we need to talk about the reason why I'm here. Javad Natal. I hear he wants to make a trade with you. That trade cannot happen, my friend," I said.

"Why not? The deal is as good as sealed. I have a beautiful shipment coming in from him," he said speaking in code.

"And that shipment is the love of my life," I said and then explained to him what happened.

"So, it seems like he was going to double-cross you. That's not good business at all. Tell me how I can fix this," he said, and we went over a plan that would leave Raven out of harm's way and make Javad and Peach suffer.

Raven

I was still in shock after my wedding. I was married to a man that I truly loved, but the man that was supposed to be my first love did the unthinkable. After finally coming to terms with the fact that I would never be able to win over Felicity, I decided to bury the hatchet and stop myself from harming her. Only to have my father snatch her anyway.

"This is so fucked up! Why is he like this?" I cried onto Ramon's shoulder.

"*Mi amor*, don't worry about a thing. I know it seems like the sky is falling but know that my umbrella will keep the pieces away from you," Ramon said using the worst analogy I had ever heard.

"First, never use that analogy again. It's horrible. And I know what is going to happen. I'm going to have to bury my father. That is, if his body is ever recovered. I know what he did is punishable by death. No women or children—ever," I said.

"I don't want to hurt you by killing your father, but he made his choice when he decided to take a friend's mate. I know you don't like Felicity, and I would never have you pretend that you do, but you have to know that what your father did could have started a war between me and one of my oldest friends," Ramon said.

"I know, babe. I mean, I really don't have any more ill feelings towards

Felicity, but that doesn't mean we're going to be taking vacations and going to the spa together. I just want some peace in my life. And I didn't even know that you and Jason were so close," I stated.

"I know you didn't. Jason and I never talk about each other with others. This has kept the feds off our radar for years. They never knew we were connected because we never let you know. I even made sure that it was okay to pursue you the way I wanted when your father dropped you off to me in Bogota," he told me.

He told me how they met as kids when their fathers did business together. Ramon and his father made many trips from Colombia to the states to visit Jason's family, and the two of them were more like brothers than friends. They both ended up taking their father's positions and making their businesses better than ever. Both of those men were smarter than I realized, and I admired Ramon even more for his honesty.

"Let's make a baby," I blurted out of my mouth faster than my brain could catch up.

"Say that one more time," he coaxed.

"You heard it the first time," I said. I was dead ass serious, too.

I never once thought that I would think about being a mom. My mom died when I was young, and my father was all I had to show me how to be a parent. He was cold and distant and that led me to think that I wasn't fit to be a mother. But suddenly, being with Ramon had me thinking otherwise. I wanted a baby with him so that I could see a miniature version of him.

"Let's start right now," Ramon said and swept me up in his arms and took me to his rooms to try and start our family.

Felicity

Things were reaching a fever pitch with Javad. He hadn't heard from Peach in a few days and he was starting to look and act like a maniac. He was constantly throwing things and on his phone trying to track her. But he would never let me too far out of his sight.

I was no longer bound, and I could walk freely around the small house he had me stuck in. There was one bedroom and a really nice bathroom. The kitchen was updated with granite countertops and stainless-steel appliances, and the kitchen was fully stocked. Wherever we were, it seemed like this was planned a while ago.

I could look out the bedroom window and see a private lake and trees, but not much else. It was almost as if this house was secluded for a reason. I knew that we couldn't be too far from Atlanta because then Javad wouldn't be able to get the money that he wanted from Jason. I just couldn't wait to get away from this man and back to my regular life.

"Mikael, my friend. I have the product that you want to buy. No, no. Peach isn't going to be with me this time. She's away on a spa retreat. This one is young and tender. She's ready to go and looks to be easy to train. I'll have your money as well, my friend," I heard Javad saying on the phone.

I heard the name Mikael before from Jason and immediately knew that nothing good was going to come out of that conversation for me. I had to figure out a way to get away from this man, and fast. The only thing stopping me was the fact that I had no idea where I was or where to go. I could get lost in the woods and really go missing.

"You need to shower and put on the clothes that I bought you. You smell god awful and I need you presentable," Javad said as soon as he hung up the phone.

"I'm not going anywhere with your ass," I spat.

"You will do as I say, bitch!" he yelled and pulled a gun from the back of his pants. I had no idea that he even had a gun on him. I put my hands up in surrender and went into the bedroom to shower and change.

I walked in the room and there was a tiny ass black dress and some come-fuck-me pumps on the bed. There was also a pair of cute fishnet stockings on the bed. I didn't like anything else that he laid out for me because I looked like a hoe about to hit the track.

I sighed and prayed that Jason was able to find me in time.

Dylan

There were only a couple of weeks left in my stay in rehab and I was really feeling like a new man. I learned a lot about myself being here and I knew that there was so much that I fucked up on in life. I ruined my career, business relationships and even destroyed my family in the process.

Instead of trying to just co-parent with Fefe, I had to come in between her relationship and cause problems. Not because I loved her, but because I felt like I owned her. I self-sabotaged my career because I wasn't happy with myself and I wanted help. I just didn't know how to ask for it. Thank God my father was in my corner the whole time. Without him, I would probably be dead somewhere.

"Dylan, what are your plans after you leave? I would recommend that you go to a sober living home for at least thirty days. It will be hard to transition from here to directly go into your regular life," my therapist Mona was advising me.

"I'm not completely sure yet, but I know that I want to get back in the studio. I have written some amazing songs here and I just want to go back to work. I just hope that I can right some of the wrongs that I made. Especially with Jason. He was there for me in the beginning, and all I did was shit on him," I said.

"Well, asking for forgiveness is one of the biggest steps towards your recovery. This will be our last session, but I am hoping nothing but the best for you," Mona said before shaking my hand and dismissing me.

I walked out of therapy feeling renewed. I saw some of the newer residents grouped up talking to each other about why they were here and why they didn't need to be here. I laughed to myself and went to my room to call Christina. I hadn't seen her since she left the center a couple of weeks back.

"Hello?" a woman answered the phone with a voice that I didn't recognize.

"Can I speak to Christina?" I asked. A bad feeling started to creep all over me when the woman started to speak again.

"I don't know how to tell you this, but my sister decided to kill herself. She's dead," she said and then ended the call just as abruptly as she told me that my friend was dead.

I sank down on my bed and held my head in my hands. I started to cry silently and hard as hell. Christina was one of the toughest people that I knew, and it just didn't feel right that she committed suicide. Then the way her sister talked about her sent my mind reeling. I was going to use my resources to look into Christina's death.

THE DAY finally came for me to be released. My dad wanted to come and pick me up, but I had other plans that didn't involve some warm and fuzzy family reunion. I was headed to Tennessee to find out what really happened to Christina. The way her sister spoke about her was off and wasn't sitting right with me. Then my father told me that some shit was going on with Felicity and that she had fallen completely off the grid since Raven's wedding. I needed answers from everyone, and no one was answering my questions.

"I really wish you would move into the sober house that I recommended," Star said as she hugged me.

"I know you want me to, but I just want to focus on my music. I promise you I won't let you down and relapse," I said, meaning every word.

"I'm holding you to that. But don't be afraid to come back if necessary. No judgements here," she said, hugging me one last time before I hopped in the waiting cab.

I had the driver take me to the airport and I purchased a ticket for Memphis. Christina was from there and I knew that she was going to go back and try to make things right with her family. I remember her telling me that she and her sister hated each other and that she wanted to figure out a way to mend fences with her.

I sat back on the plane after takeoff and managed to get a nap in. I texted my father and told him that I would talk to him in a few days. I made up some story about going in the studio and sleeping there so he wouldn't show up at my door looking for me.

"Thank you for flying Delta," the flight attendant said as I passed her on my way off the plane.

I stepped into the busy ass airport and asked for the baggage claim. After getting my luggage, I made my way out of the airport and found the taxi stand. I hopped in a cab and had him take me to the nearest hotel. I didn't need the Four Seasons, but I didn't want the Snooty Fox either.

I was dropped off at the Holiday Inn where I checked in and immediately left back out. I called for an Uber and headed to Christina's mother's house. I wanted to know what really happened because the bitch that answered the phone was on some bullshit.

I pulled up to a dilapidated house smack dead in the center of the hood and got out the car. I gingerly walked up the steps and knocked on the old door. A pretty older woman opened the door and I saw what Christina would have looked like in about twenty more years. She looked confused for a moment before she recognized me and squealed in happiness.

"Dylan James is at my door. I can't believe it! Come on in!" she exclaimed and let me in the house. The inside was completely different from the outside and if you hadn't seen it, you wouldn't believe that it was the same house.

"Mrs. Atkinson, thank you for your time. I know you think that I am some big star, but I really am just a regular guy. I met your daughter at rehab," I explained and told her everything about rehab.

"Oh, sugar, trust me I know all about my baby girl's troubles. She was the one to check herself in each time. She wanted to change so bad, but her sister made it hard for her," Christina's mother, Dot, said. She told me how all the time growing up, Christina's sister would mock her about her dark skin.

"Christina's sister made her life hell. I tried as much as I could to get Cress to ease up on her sister and just be her sister. But of course, that child is the devil herself. It wouldn't surprise me if she had something to do with my baby girl's death," she admitted to me.

"Well, I'm here and I have money and resources to really find out what happened. Something sounded off when I called Christina's phone." I told her what happened when I talked to Cress on the phone.

"I knew something wasn't right. My soul has been telling me that something was off since the police knocked on my door. They refuse to look into it. I mean we're just a black family in the hood. They don't give a fuck about us," she said as she spoke on how the laws were interpreted differently when it came to race.

"Well, they won't give me the same trouble, hopefully. Don't worry about a thing. I'll help you find out the truth." I stood up and gave Dot a hug before writing my number down.

I called an Uber to take me back to the hotel and waited inside for it to arrive. While I was waiting in the kitchen, I heard the front door open and a familiar voice call out for Dot. When the body attached to the voice walked into the kitchen, I was staring into the light skin version of Christina.

"Damn, you still fine. My sister should have hit that before she killed herself. Maybe the bitch would still be here," Cress said and grabbed a glass from the cabinet to pour some juice in.

I saw that my Uber had arrived, and I rushed out the house and jumped in my ride. The whole way back to the hotel, I was thinking about everything that had happened at Christina's mother's house. I was put off by the whole thing. Something was still off about both women. Something about Dot's story seemed too rehearsed, like she'd studied her lines.

I acted for years and made my living off making people believe the emotions that I acted out were genuine. So, when I saw heard Dot's story, my acting senses kicked in. She was lying, and I was going to find out why. I got out of the car and walked in the hotel and went into my room to rest.

As soon as I got comfortable enough to get focused, I ordered some food from Door Dash and mustered up the nerve to call on the one person I knew that wanted to fuck me up. Jason.

Jason

Word had finally gotten back to me that Javad had resurfaced with Felicity. He was bringing her to Mikael and then he was going to get a payment and try to leave the country. He also sent a message to me saying the same shit, only that he wanted twice the amount that he wanted from Mikael. It was like he was using Felicity to start a war between me and the Russians.

"My friend, he has the girl and is bringing her tonight," Mikael said while we were enjoying Frapin VIP XO cognac that he always had shipped when he traveled.

"It's about time that Jay the Jackal comes out of retirement. All these niggas got me fucked up," I said and downed the drink in my glass before signaling for the girl holding the bottle to pour me another.

I was about to speak again, but my phone chimed, indicating that I had a text message coming through. I rolled my eyes when I saw that it was Dylan, until I read the message. He let me know that he had finished rehab and wanted to come back to work for real. Then he started talking about a girl he met and how she suddenly killed herself and how it felt like it was more to it. He wanted my help and that I was the only person that could help him.

It sounded like he was really in love with this girl and I would help him as long as he wasn't after Felicity. If this would keep him from inter- fering in my shit, I would help him. Plus, this fool was a moneymaker and I refused to let my personal shit come in between me getting that bag. I shot him a text back so that he could give me everything that he knew so far.

I would shoot it over to my nigga that could hack into the CIA if he wanted to. This nigga Shaquel was a beast with the hacking shit, and I paid a lot of money to keep his ass out of jail so he could keep me informed of shit. As soon as I got the message from Dylan, I sent that over to Shaquel and his Dave East looking ass.

"Was that business or pleasure, my friend?" Mikael asked.

"Purely business. My only pleasure right now is getting wifey back and killing these two," I said as I looked Peach dead in her eyes.

I wanted her ass to see Javad get tortured to death before I put a bullet between her eyes. I was going to give her to Mikael and let him sell her ass off to the highest bidder, but that shit would never sit right with me. She was going to die because she put my girl in danger, all for fucking money.

"All you had to do was walk the fuck away and none of this shit would be happening. You are going to die. I just don't know how or when. All I know is you will watch your man die," I said in a voice that even scared myself a little.

"It's time, my friend," Mikael said. He stood up and straightened up his suit that I was sure was bulletproof.

"Get up," I told Peach. She did as I asked without a word. Mainly because I had a ball gag in her mouth.

She stumbled behind us in a dress that was so short you could see her liver, and heels so high, that I was sure that she could look Shaq in the eye. I knew what I was doing. I wanted Javad to see what it felt like to have the woman he was fucking to be looked at like a piece of meat. I was tempted to have him watch her be auctioned off before killing him, but I rarely went against my plans.

We climbed into the back of an Excursion and pulled off into the night to meet Javad at the house I used to share with Raven. This was some sick shit that this man was on. Bringing us to the place where my biggest hurt developed was a slap in the face. I was sure he was telling Felicity all about my marriage and this house.

"Don't let your emotions take over. Use your head, my friend," Mikael observed.

I was to the point if he called me "my friend" one more time, I was going to shoot myself. I understood that was the way he communicated, but that shit was on my last fucking nerve. I could speak Russian fluently, but his ass insisted on speaking English. He was my friend, but I was sick of him by now.

I saw that Raven and Ramon had pulled in behind us and they were waiting for our signal to move. I knew why we were still sitting in the cars. Mikael and I were waiting for our men to get into place. We weren't taking any chances that Javad would be able to run off into the night if things didn't go his way.

They had cut the power on the entire block, causing a blackout in the neighborhood so that we could move unnoticed. We didn't want to raise any alarms and have the police notified. Even though the police chief was on my payroll, he wouldn't be able to turn a blind eye to a neighborhood bloodbath. Because if one person saw Mikael, he would take out every single one of the neighbors without any remorse.

"It's time," Mikael said and opened up his car door.

The overhead light didn't turn on in any of the cars because we didn't want anything to alert the neighbors. I looked around and saw three trucks from the electric company at the end of the block. I knew that it wasn't the workers, but they were my guys using the vehicles as a distraction. I snatched Peach out of the truck and walked towards the house.

We hadn't made it fifty feet before shots started to ring out into the night.

"FELICITY!!!!!!!!!" I screamed before I felt something hot in my chest, and then the world went fuzzy.

To Be Continued...

AUTHOR'S NOTE

Thank you so much for reading this story. If you made it this far, then you know that this is not the end. I thought that this was going to be a two-part series, but lo and behold, these characters had more life in them. There is more drama ahead as this series moves forward. There will be so many shake-ups to get to the happily ever after. Until next time—

Stay Divine!
Tabeitha

Royalty Publishing House is now accepting manuscripts from aspiring or experienced urban romance authors!

WHAT MAY PLACE YOU ABOVE THE REST:

Heroes who are the ultimate book bae: strong-willed, maybe a little rough around the edges but willing to risk it all for the woman he loves.

Heroines who are the ultimate match: the girl next door type, not perfect - has her faults but is still a decent person. One who is willing to risk it all for the man she loves.

The rest is up to you! Just be creative, think out of the box, keep it sexy and intriguing!

If you'd like to join the Royal family, send us the first 15K words (60 pages) of your completed manuscript to submissions@royaltypublishinghouse.com

LIKE OUR PAGE!

Be sure to <u>LIKE</u> our Royalty Publishing House page on Facebook!

CPSIA information can be obtained
at www.ICGtesting.com
Printed in the USA
LVHW111450011119
636084LV00003B/446/P